Five Nights at Freddy's
FAZBEAR FRIGHTS #3
1:35 A.M.

Five Nights at Freddy's

FAZBEAR FRIGHTS #3

1:35 A.M.

BY

**SCOTT CAWTHON
ELLEY COOPER
ANDREA WAGGENER**

Scholastic Inc.

If you purchased this book without a cover, you should be aware that this book is stolen property. It was reported as "unsold and destroyed" to the publisher, and neither the author nor the publisher has received any payment for this "stripped book."

Copyright © 2020 by Scott Cawthon. All rights reserved.

Photo of TV static: © Klikk/Dreamstime

All rights reserved. Published by Scholastic Inc., *Publishers since 1920*. SCHOLASTIC and associated logos are trademarks and/or registered trademarks of Scholastic Inc.

The publisher does not have any control over and does not assume any responsibility for author or third-party websites or their content.

No part of this publication may be reproduced, stored in a retrieval system, or transmitted in any form or by any means, electronic, mechanical, photocopying, recording, or otherwise, without written permission of the publisher. For information regarding permission, write to Scholastic Inc., Attention: Permissions Department, 557 Broadway, New York, NY 10012.

This book is a work of fiction. Names, characters, places, and incidents are either the product of the author's imagination or are used fictitiously, and any resemblance to actual persons, living or dead, business establishments, events, or locales is entirely coincidental.

ISBN 978-1-338-57603-0

10 9 8 7 6 5   22 23 24

Printed in the U.S.A.

First printing 2020 • Book design by Betsy Peterschmidt

TABLE OF CONTENTS

1:35 A.M. 1
Room for One More . . . 91
The New Kid 149

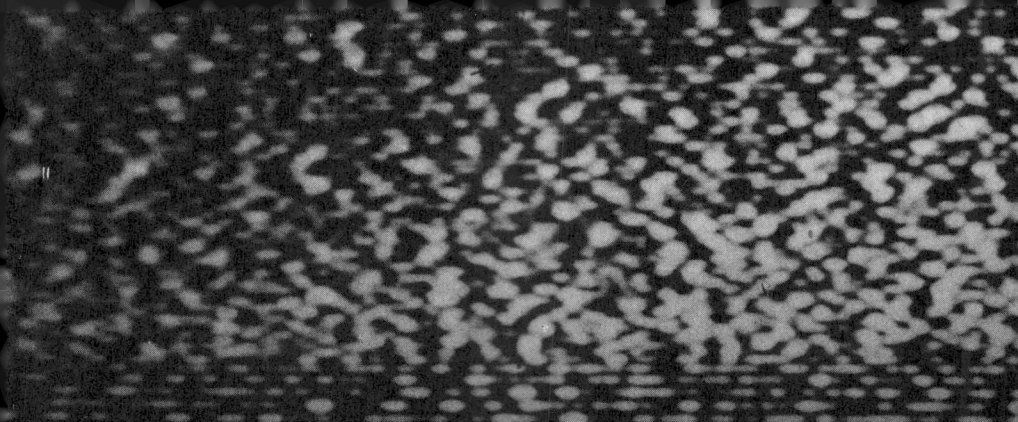

1:35 A.M.

"**Oh** hurray, buzzy, buzzy, buzzy," sang a loud tinkling voice.

The inane song reached, like a long-handled hook, into Delilah's enjoyable dream and yanked her from the blessed retreat of sleep.

"What the . . . ?" Delilah muttered as she sat up in the middle of her rumpled flannel sheets, blinking at the sun punching through gaps in her louvered blinds.

"You make me feel so perky," the singer continued.

Delilah threw her pillow at the inadequate wall that separated her apartment from the one next door. The pillow made a satisfying *thump* when it hit a framed poster depicting a serene beachy scene. Delilah looked at the poster with longing; it represented the view she wished she had.

But Delilah didn't have an ocean view. She had a view of dumpsters and the filthy backside of the twenty-four-hour diner where she worked. She didn't have serenity, either.

She had her annoying neighbor, Mary, who continued to sing at the top of her lungs: "Thank you, thank you, thank you for starting my day."

"Who sings about alarm clocks?" Delilah snapped, groaning and rubbing her eyes. It was bad enough having a singing neighbor; it was a thousand times worse that the singing neighbor made up her own stupid songs and always started her day with one about an alarm clock. Weren't alarm clocks bad enough on their own?

Speaking of which, Delilah looked at her clock. "What?" She catapulted from her bed.

Grabbing the little battery-powered digital clock, Delilah glared at its face, which read 6:25 a.m.

"What good are you?" Delilah demanded, tossing the clock onto her bright blue comforter.

Delilah had a pathological hatred of alarm clocks. It was a vestige of the ten months she spent in her last foster home nearly five years before, but life in the real world required the use of them, something Delilah was still learning to deal with. Though now she'd discovered something she hated worse than alarm clocks: *alarm clocks that didn't work.*

Delilah's phone rang. When she picked it up, she didn't wait for the caller to speak. Talking over the sound of clattering plates and a hum of voices, she said, "I know, Nate. I overslept. I can be there in thirty minutes."

"I already called in Rianne to cover. You can take her two o'clock shift."

Delilah sighed. She hated that shift. It was the really busy one.

Actually, she hated all the shifts. She hated shifts, period.

As a shift manager at the diner, she was expected to work whichever shift best fit the overall schedule. So her "days" varied from six to two, two to ten, and ten to six. Her body clock was so messed up that she was practically sleeping while she was awake and awake while she was sleeping. She lived in a state of perpetual exhaustion. Her mind was always murky, like fog had rolled in through her ears. Not only did the fog dampen her ability to think clearly, it also made it difficult for her brain to interface with her senses. It seemed as though her vision, hearing, and taste buds were always a little off.

"Delilah? Can I count on you to be here at two?" Nate barked in Delilah's ear.

1:35 A.M.

"Yeah. Yes. I'll be there."

Nate made a growling sound and hung up.

"I love you, too," Delilah said into the phone before she set it down.

Delilah looked at her queen-size bed. The thick mattress and her special memory foam pillow beckoned like a languid lover, inviting her back to bed. Delilah so wanted to give in. She loved sleep. She loved just being in her bed. It was like a cocoon—an adult version of the blanket forts she liked to build when she was little. She would spend all day in her bed if she could. She wished she could find one of those stay-at-home jobs that let her work in bed in her pajamas. It wouldn't be ideal for her employer, because she'd rather just lounge about and sleep, but it would be better for her health. She could set her own shifts if she worked for herself.

But all her searching for such a job had found nothing but work-at-home scams. The only place that would hire her after she and Richard split up was the diner. All because she had a juvie record and had dropped out of high school for reasons she barely remembered anymore. Life sucked.

Delilah looked at her useless alarm clock. No. She couldn't risk it. She had to stay awake.

But how?

Next door, Mary was on at least a third repeat of her stupid wake-up song. Delilah knew it would do no good to bang on the wall or go next door to ask Mary to keep it down. Mary wasn't cooking with all her burners. Delilah wasn't sure what was wrong with the woman; she just knew that her previous complaints had disappeared into the void that seemed to make up the mind hidden under Mary's thick gray hair.

Delilah didn't want to stay in her apartment and listen to Mary. She might as well do something useful.

Shuffling into her tiny pink-tiled bathroom, Delilah brushed her teeth and dressed in gray sweats and a red T-shirt. She figured she might as well go for a jog. It had been at least three days since she'd gotten exercise. Maybe that had something to do with the fog in her head.

Nah. She knew that wasn't true. She'd tried exercise as a solution to her constant exhaustion. It didn't seem to matter how much she worked out. Her body just didn't like bouncing from one schedule to another like a hummingbird flitting about.

"It's just because it's winter," Delilah's best friend, Harper, said. "When spring comes, you'll wake up, just like the flowers."

Delilah had doubted that, and rightfully so. Spring was here. Everything was blooming . . . except Delilah's energy levels.

But whether it would help her head or not, Delilah put on her running shoes and tucked her keys, phone, some money, driver's license, and a credit card into her running pouch, which she then hung around her neck.

1:35 A.M.

Leaving her little noisy apartment—Mary was still singing—Delilah stepped out into a carpeted hallway that smelled like bacon, coffee, and glue. What was with the glue?

Delilah snorted as she trotted down three flights of narrow, uneven steps. The super was probably fixing the wall or something. She wasn't exactly living in an upscale place.

Two sullen, slouchy teens ambled through the building's lobby as Delilah reached it. They eyed her. She ignored them, stepping through the scratched gray metal door just in time to watch the sun duck behind a fluffy white cloud.

It was one of those bright, breezy spring days that Harper loved and Delilah hated. Maybe if she lived on the coast or in a forest, she could appreciate the happy sun and the sprightly air currents. Surrounded by nature and maybe some blossoming flowers, such a day would feel right. But here?

Here in this urban conglomeration of strip malls, machine shops, car dealerships, vacant lots, and low-income housing, *bright and breezy* wasn't pleasant; it was jarring. A tiara would look more suitable on a pig.

Trying to ignore smells of rotting lettuce, exhaust, and rancid frying oil, Delilah propped her foot on the side of the empty flower planter in front of her gray-walled boxy building. Maybe it would feel more like spring if the planters were growing flowers instead of rocks. Delilah stretched, then shook her head at her negativity.

"You know better," she scolded herself.

Setting off at a medium-paced jog, Delilah pointed herself north, which would take her through the nearest housing area, where she could run past houses and trees instead of struggling businesses and cars.

She needed to get out of this dark spiral she was in. She'd had enough therapy when she was in her teens to know that she had an "obsessive personality"; once she latched onto a perspective, there was no unlatching her. Right now, she was stuck on the idea that her life sucked. It was going to continue to suck if she didn't pick a new idea.

As her feet met the uneven sidewalk, Delilah tried to clear the fog from her brain by thinking happy thoughts. "Every day, I'm getting better and better," she chanted. After ten rounds or so of this affirmation, she was starting to feel snarly. So she traded affirmations for an image of the life she wanted to be living. That made her think of the life she *had* been living with Richard, which just dropped her further into the negativity pit.

When Richard decided he wanted to replace his dark-haired, dark-eyed Mrs. with a blonde, blue-eyed wife, Delilah didn't have many options. She'd signed a prenuptial agreement before marrying Richard. She had nothing going into the marriage, and she got nothing in the divorce. Well, not *nothing*. She received enough of a settlement to get her an apartment, some secondhand furniture, and her fifteen-year-old tan compact sedan. She got these after she found the one place that was willing to hire her and train her. Given her stunning résumé of "completed half of twelfth grade," "babysat," and "worked in a fast-food restaurant," she was lucky to get what she got. And, awful hours aside, the job had been good to her. Nate had sent her to management training, and she had climbed the ladder from server to shift manager in just a few months. At twenty-three, she was the youngest shift manager in the restaurant.

"See?" Delilah panted. "Things are looking up."

She clung to that tenuously positive thought as she jogged through the ratty old neighborhood that backed onto an industrial park. The neighborhood was too run-down to be called pretty, but it was filled with beautiful old maple trees and tall sinewy poplars that swayed in the gentle wind coming up the street. All the trees were filled with light-green new growth. The tender leaves encouraged more hopeful thoughts, if only for a minute or two.

She wondered if the people who lived in the area ever let the trees inspire them. Looking around, she doubted it. A few listless kids were waiting for the yellow school buses that belched diesel fumes as they came chugging up behind Delilah. An old guy with a shiny bald head mowed a yard full of weeds, and a woman whose attitude appeared to be worse than Delilah's stood on her front porch glaring into a coffee mug.

Delilah decided she'd had enough of the neighborhood, and enough of her run, for that matter. She looped around a defunct car parts store and aimed for home.

Home.

If only it *was* home. But her apartment wasn't home. She'd had two homes in her life. One she shared with her parents, until they died when she was eleven. The foster "homes" she'd lived in after that were nothing more than places to bide her time. Her other home was with Richard. Now she just had a place where she slept, and she never got to sleep enough.

Lately, it felt like life was just one annoying sleep interruption after another, like the world was an alarm that kept going off and waking her from her dreams, the only place she could find a truly happy thought.

Back in her apartment, Delilah did her best to ignore her mostly empty pale-green walls—she hadn't gotten up the *oomph* to repaint since she'd moved in. She took off her shoes and put them neatly by the front door. She crossed to her well-worn beige leather loveseat and straightened the green-and-yellow afghan draped over its back. Delilah didn't like the afghan, but Harper had crocheted it for her. One day, Harper had dropped by and was crushed when she didn't see the afghan. After that, Delilah had left it out.

"You just have to be careful to tuck in the wonky bits," Harper told Delilah when she presented the gift. Given

1:35 A.M.

that there were many such bits, proper tucking was challenging.

Mary continued warbling next door as Delilah peeled off her sweaty T-shirt and opened the cabinet where she kept her stash of cookies. The cabinet was empty. Of course.

Sighing, Delilah opened her refrigerator. She knew that was a futile action because she didn't cook and therefore kept nothing in the fridge but bottled water, apple juice, and half-eaten carryout food from the diner. One of the perks of working at the diner was she got two free meals every shift. That kept her pretty well fed. So all she really needed were her cookies, milk, some protein bars, and frozen dinners for the nights she didn't work. The refrigerator revealed that she needed not just cookies but milk, too.

Mary's voice wafted through the wall. "Spring has sprung and worms have come . . ."

"Yes, that's what I'm afraid of, Mary," Delilah said.

She couldn't stay here.

Striding into her small bathroom, Delilah took a lukewarm shower, then dressed in brown leggings and a gold-and-black plaid jacket. She avoided looking in the mirror while she dried her wavy shoulder-length hair. Delilah didn't wear makeup anymore. Rather than spend money on cosmetics that got her unwanted male attention, she left her face bare and put the extra dollars in her savings account. Even without makeup, Delilah was pretty enough to turn heads. A modeling agency she applied to once told her she was just a large chin shy of having classically beautiful features. Two agencies had given her the names of plastic surgeons and told her to come back after she had a little chin and jaw work done.

Delilah figured if she wasn't going to put on makeup, why look in the mirror? She knew what she looked like, and lately, she wasn't too keen on meeting her own gaze. She saw something there that scared her, something that made her wonder what her future held.

Next door, Mary was singing at the top of her lungs about visiting Mars. "You go, Mary," Delilah said, wishing Mary would go to Mars . . . and not come back.

Grabbing her purse, Delilah headed for her car. She figured she could get to the store, get some cookies and milk, and still come back in time to take a little nap before work.

After a visit to the grocery store replenished her oatmeal cookie stash and her milk supply, Delilah left the store from the rear of the parking lot. She liked weaving her way back to the apartment on quiet neighborhood roads instead of the congested four lanes that ran through the heart of the industrial and retail splat she lived in.

This neighborhood was a little nicer than the one she ran through. It had bigger houses, greener lawns, and newer cars. The trade-off was that the older neighborhood had those big maple and poplar trees, and this new

1:35 A.M.

neighborhood had runty cherry trees. She had to admit that the pink blossoms were pretty, though.

Turning the corner next to a particularly flowery tree, Delilah spotted a garage sale sign. Its arrow pointed straight ahead, so, on a whim, she went that way. Two more signs directed her to take right turns, and eventually, she found herself in front of a two-story Spanish-style home looming over several card tables piled high with household merchandise.

Delilah couldn't help herself. She had to stop.

Just as Delilah had a thing about getting stuck in a thought pattern, she had a thing about garage sales. She'd been hooked on them since she was a teen. One of her therapists, Ali, had a theory about it. Ali thought Delilah loved garage sales because they gave her glimpses into family life. They reminded her of what "normal" looked like.

Delilah wasn't an obsessive garage sale shopper. Yes, she did occasionally buy—she'd gotten all her current furniture from garage sales. Mostly, though, Delilah was a garage sale watcher, an archaeologist of household items, a "stuff" private eye. She wanted to know what people used, what they collected, what they loved, and what they didn't want to keep around anymore. It entertained her.

Figuring her milk could sit in the car for fifteen minutes or so, Delilah pulled her car behind a dirty red pickup. The pickup and a powder-blue Cadillac were the only cars parked in front of the house. Just two people wandered among the tables. One person was a heavyset woman who seemed intent on kitchenware. The other was a slight young man who was browsing piles of books and records. Delilah nodded at them both and also at the middle-aged woman who sat next to a picnic table that held a metal cash box, a pad of paper, and a calculator.

"Welcome," the woman called out. She had short, spiky brown hair, and her eyes were encircled in heavy black eyeliner. She wore a yellow running suit, and she carried a butterscotch-colored Chihuahua that was so quiet and docile, Delilah began to wonder whether it was real. But when she stepped up to pet it, the dog wagged its tail.

"This is Mumford," the woman said.

"Hello, Mumford." Delilah scratched Mumford behind the ears, becoming Mumford's new best friend.

Strolling away from Mumford and his human, Delilah explored the intriguing piles on each table. She poked through small appliances, tools, games, puzzles, electronics, and clothes, finding a black leather jacket that intrigued her until she sniffed it and got a nose full of stale mothballs. Wandering to the next table, she found herself in the "toy section." A glance at a pile of fashion dolls darkened her already precarious mood because the dolls reminded her of how impossible it was to prevent other foster kids from playing with her stuff when she was growing up. Blocks made her think of a little foster brother she'd gotten close to in foster home number three, only to lose him to adoption a week before she was moved to a different home. She was getting ready to walk away from the table, in search of home decor items, when her gaze landed on a different doll.

With brown curly hair, big dark eyes, and plump pink cheeks, the doll looked almost exactly like the baby Delilah had envisioned having someday with Richard. At the start of their marriage, her baby was as real to her as anything in the physical world. She'd been sure she was going to be a mother, so sure that she named the baby before the baby was even conceived. Her name would be Emma.

Intrigued, Delilah circled the table to get closer to the doll. Tucked in a large wooden box full of plush toys and electronic gadgets, the pretty baby face was partially shadowed by the doll's blue hat. The hat's wide brim, fringed in pink ruffles, looked incongruous wedged between a game console and what looked like a remote-control airplane. Delilah had to shift both items to free the doll, which was about two feet tall.

Wearing a puffy-sleeved, 1980s-era bright blue full-skirted dress with pink ruffled trim and a big bow around the waist, the doll was much heavier than Delilah expected her to be. When she examined the doll, Delilah realized this was because the doll was electronic.

Delilah reached for the bright pink tag and instructional

booklet that hung from the doll's wrist. "My name is Ella," the tag read.

Ella. So close to Emma. Delilah felt an odd tingle slither through her body. How weird was that? A doll that looked like her long-desired baby and a name that was far too close to be a coincidence. Although it had to be a coincidence, didn't it?

Delilah opened the little booklet. Her eyes widened. *Wow.* This was a high-tech doll.

According to the booklet, Ella was a "helper doll" manufactured by Fazbear Entertainment. "Fazbear Entertainment," Delilah whispered. She'd never heard of it.

The booklet had a list of what Ella was designed for, and the list was impressive. Ella could do all sorts of things. She could keep time and serve as an alarm clock, manage appointments, keep track of lists, take photos, read stories, sing songs, and even serve drinks. *Serve drinks?* Delilah shook her head.

Looking around, Delilah was relieved to see that no one was paying attention to her interest in the doll. Mumford's mom was helping the young man looking at records. The heavyset woman was busy piling china plates next to the metal cash box. No one else had shown up.

Delilah kept reading. Ella, the booklet said, could test the pH levels in water and she could also do personality assessments when you answered her programmed list of 200 questions. How was it possible for an old toy to be that sophisticated?

1:35 A.M.

Both Ella's design and that of her booklet suggested that her clothing matched her year of manufacture. She was not new, not even close. Did she really do all of these things?

Delilah turned Ella over, and she found a note pinned to Ella's dress. The note explained that the only one of Ella's functions that worked was the alarm clock. Delilah flipped Ella again, and she saw that Ella had a small digital clock embedded in her chest. Concentrating on following the instructions, Delilah attempted to activate the alarm clock feature by pressing a sequence of little buttons found on Ella's round belly.

Delilah nearly dropped poor Ella when the last button she pushed made Ella's eyes bolt open. She sucked in her breath at the snapping sound, and her heartbeat quadrupled in a nanosecond when Ella went from asleep to awake in an instant.

Delilah held Ella out in front of her. Well, she *did* need an alarm clock. She checked the little white price tag stuck to the back of Ella's neck. Not too bad. Delilah could handle that. And maybe she could get the price down. Her hundreds of garage sale visits had turned her into a pretty good haggler.

Delilah picked up Ella and headed toward Mumford and his mom, who were both back behind the cash box. The young man was loading a box of records into his pickup.

"Will you shave fifteen dollars off this price?" Delilah asked. "Since she has only one function?"

The woman held out a hand with bright red fingernails. She turned Ella over, looked at the price, then looked up at Delilah, who tried to look eager and poor at the same time. "Okay. Sure. I can do that."

Delilah grinned. "Great."

As she paid, she instructed herself to notice that her day did indeed get better as it went along. It didn't suck to have a nice run, buy more cookies, and find a very cool high-tech doll for a good price at a garage sale. Ella would make a cool conversation piece to perch on Delilah's old oak coffee table. Harper was going to love Ella.

And now Delilah had a working alarm clock! She could go home, take a nap, and still have a way to be sure she got up in time for work. Yep. Things were looking up. Maybe she could get off the "life sucks" track after all.

Back in her apartment, Delilah set Ella on her nightstand, under her white ginger jar lamp. Ella, with her poofy dress all fluffed up and spread out around her, looked good there, content even. Actually, she looked a little pleased with herself, which was, of course, a projection because Ella wasn't even *aware* of herself. It was Delilah who was pleased with herself. She was proud for finding a way to turn the day around. She'd gotten past her funk. That was pretty impressive.

Delilah checked her watch and set Ella's clock to match that time. It was barely 11:30 a.m., so Delilah was going to be able to grab a couple hours of sleep. Setting Ella's alarm

1:35 A.M.

for 1:35 p.m., Delilah smoothed her sheets and blanket and lay down on top of them, pulling up the comforter to her chin, not because it was cold in her apartment but because it made her feel secure. Thankful that Mary was either asleep herself, was out running errands, or had ruined her vocal cords with too much singing, Delilah lay back and let herself ride the currents of drowsiness into blissful unconsciousness.

The phone blasted through Delilah's peace like a rocket shattering monastery walls. She shot upright and grabbed for her phone, chastising herself for not shutting it off so her nap wouldn't be interrupted.

"What?" she snarled.

"Where the hell are you?" Nate snarled right back.

"Huh? It's . . ." Delilah looked at Ella. Ella's clock read 2:25 p.m. "Oh crap."

"You better be here in fifteen minutes or don't ever be here again."

Delilah pulled the phone from her ear just in time to avoid the *CLAP* she knew was coming. Nate used an old-fashioned corded phone, the kind with the metal hook for the receiver. He expressed himself via the force with which he replaced the phone on its hook after a call. He was pissed.

Delilah ran into her bathroom, tearing off her clothes as she went. She splashed water on her face. Running a brush through her hair, she trotted back into the bedroom, yanked on her dark-blue uniform dress, and grabbed her work shoes, ugly black no-slips Nate made all the employees wear. As she laced them up, her gaze landed on Ella.

"Well, you're a disappointment," she told the doll.

Ella looked back at her through thick lashes. One of her curls had fallen over an eye. She almost looked mischievous.

No wonder the doll was so cheap. The only thing that worked was the clock in the middle of Ella's chest. But without the alarm function, what good was the clock? Ella was still a pretty doll, and she still looked like Delilah's long-desired baby, but now she was more a reminder of Delilah's frustration than anything else.

Finishing with her shoes, Delilah snatched Ella from the nightstand. For a second, she marveled at the realism of Ella's baby-soft "skin." But then she strode into the living room, grabbed her purse, and headed out the door. Jogging down the hall to the stairs, Delilah shook her head when she heard Mary belt out, "I love the big, bright world."

Outside, the sun had ceded the sky to a ceiling of low-hanging clouds spitting fat raindrops. Delilah paused to hold the door open for two elderly ladies who took an excruciatingly long time to go inside. Then she tore around the side of the building, heading for the dumpsters.

Three green hulking dumpsters sat like a trio of trolls at the edge of the apartment building's parking lot. Two were

1:35 A.M.

open. One was closed. Delilah aimed toward the second open dumpster, and she swung Ella in an arc, releasing Ella's hand at the apex of the curve. Ella flew through the intermittent precipitation and landed with a reverberating metallic *thud* in one of the open dumpsters. Delilah winced a little at the sound, feeling guilty for tossing out a doll that looked just like her baby, a doll with surprisingly real-feeling hands.

Delilah didn't see which dumpster Ella landed in because Nate appeared in the diner's back doorway. Delilah waved at him.

"You late because you were playing with your dolly?" he called out.

"Very funny." Delilah ran toward the diner and reached the door just as the raindrops turned into rain sheets.

Nate stepped back to let her by, then closed the door on what was now a downpour. Delilah got a whiff of Nate's aftershave, a subtle scent of whiskey, which he was inordinately proud of. "Manly, don't you think?" he asked the first time he tried the new product. Delilah had to admit it was.

Defying the stereotype of the typical diner owner, Nate was tall, fit, good-looking, and well groomed. About fifty, he had short graying black hair and a tidy, close-trimmed beard. He also had pewter-gray eyes that could impale you with his displeasure. He was aiming those eyes at Delilah now.

"You're lucky you're good and the customers love you,"

he said. "But you need to get a handle on your tardiness. I can't let you slide forever."

"I know. I know. I'm trying."

"That you are."

Delilah's shift went quickly. That was the upside of working the two to ten. The rush could kick your butt, but at least time flew by.

Delilah got back to her apartment about 10:30 p.m., thankfully missing one of Mary's good-night songs. The building was pretty quiet. All Delilah could hear was rap music coming from one of the apartments at the end of the hall and the sound of laughter coming from a TV on the floor above.

Closing her door on what smelled like burned Brussels sprouts, Delilah hoped the noxious odor wouldn't follow her, and it didn't. Her apartment smelled like pine cleaner and oranges. It smelled better than Delilah, who smelled like grease, as she always did at the end of a shift.

Peeling off her clothes, she deposited them inside the cedar chest that sat by her door. The chest, combined with a charcoal air-purifying bag tucked inside of it, solved the grease-smell problem she'd had for weeks when she first got the diner job.

In the shower, Delilah washed off the rest of the grease smell. Then she pulled on a red long-sleeved nightshirt and settled in bed with half a container of beef stroganoff and green beans. The cook who worked the two-to-ten shift was the best one Nate had. The stroganoff was great. While she ate, Delilah watched the rerun of a comedy show on the old TV sitting on top of her antique maple dresser. The show didn't make her laugh. It didn't even make her smile. It just helped her feel less lonely while she ate.

About 11:30 p.m., Delilah set her empty Styrofoam container atop a pile of home decor magazines on her nightstand. She turned off her ginger lamp and curled up on her side. The streetlights that hovered over the parking lot outside cast sinister distorted shadows throughout her room. They looked like giant bony fingers reaching toward the bed.

Delilah closed her eyes and willed sleep to come quickly . . . which it did.

It ended just as quickly.

Delilah's eyes shot open. Her non-alarm clock's lit face told her it was 1:35 a.m.

She sat up and looked around.

What had awakened her?

Looking toward her window, she rubbed her eyes. It had been a sound, some kind of intrusive sound coming from outside her window. Had it been a ringing sound? A buzzing sound?

Delilah tilted her head, listening. She could hear nothing but the whoosh of cars on the road.

She looked back at the clock. It was now 1:36 a.m.

Wait. She'd woken at 1:35 a.m.

She'd set the doll's alarm for 1:35. What if she'd missed the a.m./p.m. settings? "Oops," she whispered. "Sorry, Ella."

Delilah thought about going outside to retrieve the possibly-still-working doll, but she was too tired. She'd look in the morning.

Delilah snuggled under the covers and went back to sleep.

"You threw it away?" Harper drew in her chin, raised an eyebrow, and quirked her mouth in her "What were you thinking?" expression.

"I thought it was broken."

"Yeah, but it could be a collectible. It could be worth something." Harper's huge blue eyes lit up at the idea of dollar signs. Delilah could almost see a calculator totaling imaginary amounts in Harper's mind.

Delilah and Harper sat at an elevated round table in Harper's favorite espresso place. Delilah sipped cinnamon tea. Harper was drinking some kind of fancy quadruple espresso. Harper was addicted to coffee.

The espresso place was a brick-walled narrow space with lots of stainless steel and chrome and very little wood. At just before 11:00 a.m., it wasn't very crowded. A dark-skinned woman with pigtails sat at one table concentrating on whatever was on her laptop, and an elderly man munched on a muffin while reading the paper. Behind the counter, machines fizzed and spit.

1:35 A.M.

"Haven't I taught you anything?" Harper asked. "Always try to sell it before you toss it. Remember?"

"I was late for work. I was a little stressed."

"You need to learn to meditate."

"Then I'd miss work because I got lost in meditation."

Harper laughed. And everyone in the place turned to look at her. Harper's laugh was like a resounding sea lion bark. You could tell how funny she thought something was by the number of barks. Delilah's comment warranted just one.

"How do you like the new play?" Delilah asked.

"It's yippy skippy fun. My lines are all crap. But I love-love my character."

Delilah smiled.

Harper had been Delilah's best friend for almost six years, ever since the two girls landed in foster care together. Determined that the foster home would be their last, they'd teamed up to help each other survive the regimented structure imposed by Gerald, the ex-military husband of the couple who'd taken them in.

Whenever Gerald admonished them for not adhering to his schedule, reminding them that this had to happen at 0500 and that had to happen at 0610, Harper would mumble something like, "And you can jump off a cliff at oh-screw-you-hundred."

She made Delilah laugh, which helped her survive.

Complete opposites in both looks and personality, Harper and Delilah probably would never have been friends if they hadn't been thrown into scheduling hell together. However, they made their friendship work. When Harper announced her mischievous plan for getting a famous playwright to cast her in his plays, Delilah just said, "Be safe." When Delilah said she was going to marry her knight in shining armor and have babies, Harper just said, "Don't sign a prenup." Harper followed Delilah's advice and had the grace not to say, "I told you so" when Delilah failed to follow hers.

"I think you should look for her," Harper said.

"What?"

"Ella. I think you should look for her." Harper toyed with one of the dozen or so blonde braids she had coiled around her head. Wearing heavy colorful makeup and a skintight green dress, she had an exotic Medusa look going on.

"Because she might be worth something." Delilah nodded.

"It's not just that. You said she looked like the baby you thought you were going to have. That's a pretty bizarre thing, don't you think? That you'd find a doll that looks like this imaginary baby? What if she's some kind of sign?"

"You know I don't believe in signs."

"Maybe you should."

Delilah shrugged, and they spent the rest of their visit talking about Harper's play and Harper's latest boyfriend. Then they reminded each other, as they always did, of the hell they'd escaped.

1:35 A.M.

"No, you cannot use the bathroom. Not until 0945. That's your scheduled time to urinate," Harper intoned. She did great impersonations, and she had Gerald nailed. She could also, eerily, mimic the alarm Gerald had used to signal every scheduled event in the household. The alarm was a sort of cross between a ring, a buzz, and a siren. Delilah always covered her ears when Harper felt compelled to impersonate it.

Richard once asked Delilah why she and Harper needed to relive their past regularly. She said, "It reminds us of how good things are now, even when they seem not so good. Anything is better than living with Gerald."

As it always did when Delilah and Harper were together, time disappeared. When Delilah went out to her car, she realized she barely had time to get home and get changed before her shift.

"Why are you being so nice to me?" Delilah asked Nate when she arrived for her two to ten.

She stood in front of the schedule posted on the bulletin board in the employee break room. Nate had scheduled Delilah for the two-to-ten shift for a full week in a row. She couldn't remember the last time she'd worked the same shift for a week. And this shift was especially good right now because as long as she went to bed within a couple hours after ending her shift, she'd wake up in plenty of time for work. She wouldn't even need an alarm clock. She could put up with the evening rush in exchange for decent sleep.

Nate looked up from doing his daily paperwork at the round table by the bulletin board. "It's in my best interests. I like it when you show up on time for work."

"Well, it's easier to show up on time to work when my body can figure out what time it is," Delilah said.

"Wuss."

"Slave driver."

"Whiner."

"Meany."

Delilah started her shift as close to happy as she'd been in some time. Work was going well. When Nate teased, Nate was happy. When Nate was happy, things ran smoothly.

Delilah had such a good time at work that she came back to the apartment in a good mood. She ate meat loaf and broccoli in a good mood, and she went to sleep in a good mood. The good mood disappeared, though, when she sat up in bed, her muscles rigid, listening.

Who was whispering?

Someone was whispering. Delilah could hear indecipherable sibilant words coming from—from where?

Wide awake, she looked at her clock. It was 1:35 a.m.

Again?

Delilah strained to understand the whispers. But they stopped. Now all she could hear were cars on the road.

Where did that whispering come from?

Ella!

It had to be.

Harper was right. Delilah should have looked for Ella.

1:35 A.M.

She should have checked, not because Ella might have been valuable or because she was a sign but because apparently her alarm was still going off at 1:35 a.m. But Delilah hadn't had time before she went to work. She'd check today for sure. She couldn't believe Ella's alarm was so powerful she could hear it from here, but then again, wasn't Mary's singing enough painful proof of the apartment's thin walls?

Delilah lay back down and closed her eyes. Ella's face filled her inner vision. Delilah opened her eyes. She sat up again.

I'm not going to get any sleep until I find her, she thought.

Delilah got up and pulled on sweats. Stuffing her feet in a pair of slip-on clogs, she reached in her nightstand drawer for a flashlight. The dumpsters were well lit, but if Ella was partially buried, Delilah might have trouble spotting her.

Throwing on an ugly multicolored cardigan Harper had crocheted for her, Delilah left her apartment, went down the silent hallway and stairs, and exited the building. Outside, the air was chilly, but the sky was clear. A few stars even managed to shine through the frothy glow of the urban night.

Delilah paused just outside the building and looked around to be sure she was alone. She was.

Padding around the building, she headed for the dumpsters. The yawning green trash bins sat ugly and under the spotlights of the streetlamps and the diner's floodlights. One of the two that had been open before was closed, and the one that had been closed was open. They all looked a little askew, like they'd been moved around.

Great. If they'd been moved, finding Ella would be like playing a game of hat trick. This might take longer than Delilah had envisioned.

Glancing around again, Delilah shrugged. She might as well get it over with.

Approaching the middle dumpster, the one she thought she'd thrown Ella into, Delilah lifted the lid, stood on her tiptoes, and shone the light down inside. The light landed on a mound of plastic garbage bags, a ratty old blanket, a smattering of takeout containers, and a sprinkling of empty cans. Her light didn't reveal the obnoxious smell of dirty diapers that Delilah's nose discovered as soon as she opened the lid. Delilah gently closed the lid, careful not to let it clang shut. If Ella was in this dumpster, she was buried.

Delilah decided she'd rather check the other two dumpsters first before diving into any of them. So she did her tiptoe-light-aiming routine first at the open one that she thought had also been open when she chucked Ella into a dumpster. The only thing that set this dumpster apart from the first one Delilah looked at was a couple dozen old paperbacks cascading over the piles of stuffed garbage bags. Delilah was tempted to take one of them, a murder mystery, but it had a suspicious red stain on it. She didn't want to know what the stain was.

The last dumpster Delilah checked was the one she was

pretty sure had been closed when she'd tossed away Ella. So she wasn't surprised to find more of the same kind of trash and no sign of Ella.

Stymied, Delilah turned off her flashlight and thought for a moment. Did she really have to get in these dumpsters and dig for Ella? She didn't know for sure that it was Ella waking her up. For all she knew it was Mary singing some dumb middle-of-the-night song or a cat in heat.

Yeah, but why did she get awakened precisely at 1:35 a.m. both last night and tonight? Coincidence? It was possible, wasn't it? Harper once went through this period when she kept waking up at 3:33 a.m., and then she saw 333 everywhere for a couple months. Harper researched the number and found out it was some kind of spiritual sign.

What if 135 was a spiritual sign just for Delilah?

She snorted and turned her back on the dumpsters. Now she was just being silly. She headed back to the front of the building. She'd stick with the coincidence theory for now. It was easier and less smelly than assuming Ella was the problem.

The coincidence explanation got strained when Delilah awoke at 1:35 a.m. for the third night in a row. This time, she was *sure* there had been a sound against her window. Had it been a scratching sound? A tapping?

Whatever it was, it had been ominous enough that Delilah immediately grabbed her flashlight and aimed it at her blinds. Then after staring at her unmoving blinds for a minute, she got up the courage to tiptoe across the room and look behind them.

Nothing was at the window. And down below in the parking lot, the dumpsters hadn't moved from the positions they'd been in the night before.

Delilah blew out air. She was going to have to search every one of those dumpsters.

Should she wait for daylight? That would make it easier, wouldn't it? And if someone asked what she was doing, she'd answer truthfully that she threw out something she shouldn't have thrown out.

Delilah left the window and took a step toward her bed. She stopped. What day was it?

Working all sorts of weird shifts, Delilah rarely knew what day of the week it was. She thought for a second. Wednesday.

"Well, crap," she grumbled.

The dumpsters were emptied on Thursday mornings, early. If she waited, Ella would be gone.

But wait, that was a good thing, right? If Ella was gone, her alarm couldn't go off and wake up Delilah. Delilah didn't think Ella was worth anything, and she was sure Ella's resemblance to Emma was a fluke. There was no reason why Delilah should have to climb through stinky trash. She could just let the garbage truck take her problem away.

Delilah smiled and got back in bed.

1:35 A.M.

★ ★ ★

Thursday night—or rather, Friday early morning—Delilah's eyes opened to see 1:35 a.m. . . . again. She was immediately fully alert. Her heart beat loudly, fast and steady like a driving beat on a timpani. This manic pace wasn't caused only by the time. It was also a reaction to Delilah's disturbingly strong feeling that something was under her bed. Something was *moving* under her bed.

But that couldn't be.

Could it?

Delilah listened. She didn't hear anything at first, but then she wondered if she was hearing a scuttling sound on the carpet under her bed.

She sat up and started to swing a leg over the side of the bed. She stopped. What if something *was* under there? It could grab her foot!

Quickly pulling her foot back under the covers, Delilah reached out and turned on her nightstand lamp.

As soon as her room was lit, she leaned over and checked the floor all around her bed. She saw nothing but the tan-and-cream-colored carpet she'd gotten at a yard sale.

She'd just imagined the sound.

Or something was still under her bed.

Delilah reached for her nightstand drawer. She grabbed her flashlight, turned it on, took a deep breath, then hung over the bed and shined the light beneath it. Nothing was there.

Okay, this was getting crazy. It was four nights in a row. It *had* to be Ella.

But the dumpsters had been emptied.

Delilah crossed her legs and rubbed her arms. They were covered with goose bumps.

What if the trash collectors didn't completely empty the dumpsters? Or what if Ella fell out as the bin was being emptied?

Delilah had to check, and she had to check *now*. She needed to know.

So repeating her steps from two nights before, Delilah went out to the dumpsters with her flashlight. Tonight, they were all closed. They usually were after trash pickup on Thursdays.

Delilah approached the dumpsters in order, from right to left. She lifted three lids and shined her light into three nearly empty bins. All she found were two bags of household trash, a bag of dirty diapers (and its corresponding nasty odor), a broken lamp, and a sad pile of old men's clothing. The only thing that could have hidden Ella was the pile of clothing, so Delilah, holding her breath, hung over the edge of the dumpster that had the clothing and used her flashlight to poke around in the pile. The only thing under the clothes were more clothes.

Delilah picked her way between the dumpsters and around the area surrounding them. She shined her flashlight into every dark nook or cranny she spotted. No Ella.

The doll was gone. For sure. She wasn't here.

She couldn't be what was waking Delilah up at 1:35 a.m.

So what was?

Delilah woke at 10:10 the next morning, and the first thing she did when she got up, besides covering her ears so she wouldn't hear Mary singing about dusting books, was call Harper and ask her to come by. She woke Harper up, but Harper never let stuff like that bother her.

"Sure, I'll be there in a bit," she chirped.

When Harper arrived, she dropped her voluminous sack-style leather purse on the floor, flopped onto the love seat, and said, "What's the problem?"

"How do you know there's a problem?" Delilah sat down next to her.

"You don't normally ask me to come over."

Oh yeah. Delilah had basically summoned her friend. That showed how rattled she was.

"I have a question," Delilah said.

"Must be a good one."

"Did you rescue Ella from the dumpster yesterday?"

"What?"

Mary sang out, "Because I feel fizzy yey."

Harper grinned. She liked Mary's songs.

"The doll. Ella. Did you get her out of the dumpster?"

Harper ruffled her eyebrows. "Why would I do that?"

"You said she could be worth something."

"Well, she could, but she's your doll. Not mine. If I was going to look for her, I'd tell you."

Delilah rubbed her face with her hands. Yeah, she should have known that.

"Why are you asking? Did you look and not find her?"

"Yeah, I looked, sort of. I didn't dig through the trash. But then the dumpsters were emptied."

"Okay. So Ella is gone. What's the big?"

Delilah hadn't told Harper about being wakened at 1:35 a.m. every morning. She'd just told her about finding the doll and throwing it out when it didn't work. She couldn't think of a way to tell Harper about waking up at the same time four nights in a row without sounding like she was overreacting. Besides, Harper would just talk about signs again if Delilah told her.

"Since I'm here, you wanna go get some lunch?" Harper asked.

Delilah waved good-bye to Harper with relief. She was glad the lunch was over because in the middle of it, she'd come up with an idea. Now, she could finally act on it.

Pointing her car in the direction of the newer neighborhood with the runty cherry trees, she went in search of the house where she'd found the garage sale . . . and Ella. She planned to get some answers about the doll from the doll's previous owner.

Without signs to direct her, Delilah missed a turn and had to backtrack. Eventually, though, she pulled up in front of the Spanish-style house where she'd met Mumford, the friendly Chihuahua.

But Mumford wasn't home. Nobody was.

Even though Delilah could see from the street that the bare windows revealed vacant rooms in the house, she pulled into the empty driveway and got out of her car.

Inhaling the still, humid air, she wrinkled her nose at a smell that reminded her of rotting leaves. The neighborhood was unusually silent. The only thing she heard was a lone dog barking in the distance.

This was the house, wasn't it? She studied it, then turned and looked at the surrounding houses. Yes, this was it.

"Weird," she said aloud.

But was it?

After all, the woman who'd lived here had been having a garage sale. People did that before they moved, right? Delilah couldn't read anything into the fact that there was no trace of anyone or anything at this place where she'd found Ella.

So why did it feel portentous?

Hoping she might stumble over some clue to where Mumford and the woman with the spiky hair might have gone, Delilah circled the house and peeked in windows. She found nothing. The house was completely empty but for a single wadded-up paper towel on the counter in the kitchen. All Delilah got from her exploration was a creepy coil of unease that wrapped itself around her chest and didn't leave, even after she practically ran for her car and drove away as fast as she could.

Back in her apartment, Delilah ate enough cookies and milk to dissipate the disquiet she'd taken away from the empty house.

"Okay," she said. "Plan B."

Setting up her laptop in her bed, Delilah got comfy. She checked her watch. She had about forty-five minutes before she had to go to work. Plenty of time, she hoped.

Next door, Mary was singing about mushrooms, but Delilah didn't care. She was on a mission. She figured she could find information about Ella on the Internet.

She started her web search with "Ella doll." She was afraid that would be too general, but one of the millions of results gave her some information. Production of the Ella doll, Delilah discovered, was discontinued for undisclosed reasons. Jumping off from that fact, she tried to find out more about the doll, but she kept bumping into the same useless information or the text of the instruction booklet she'd already read.

Running out of time, she began trying crazy searches: "haunted Ella doll," "broken Ella doll," "unique Ella doll," "defective Ella doll," "special Ella doll." These searches took her into a lot of pointless blogs that had nothing to do with *the* Ella doll. But one of the searches for "special Ella doll" led her to an online ad posted by a user named Phineas who was trying to find one of the dolls. His ad referenced the "special Ella doll" and said he was willing to pay a premium for the doll's energy. Whatever that meant.

Delilah checked her watch. She had to get to work.

So much for her clever ideas. All they'd done was put her more on edge than she already was.

Three more nights. Three more 1:35 a.m. awakenings.

One night, Delilah had awakened certain that she was being watched. Every hair on her body had bristled like little antennae telling her she was under scrutiny. In her mind's eye, she saw Ella's huge dark eyes boring into her soul. When she lunged for her light, she thought something touched her arm. But the light revealed she was alone.

The next night, Delilah heard a rustling sound so faint it shouldn't even have been noticeable. But it still jolted Delilah from sleep. When she opened her eyes, the sound got louder. It was coming from her closet, as if someone was rifling through her clothes. Fumbling for her light, Delilah got up, strode to her closet door, and flung it open. The closet contained nothing but her clothes and shoes.

The next night, a rapping sound woke up Delilah. In her dream, the rapping came from a woodpecker. When she was awake, though, she realized the rapping was coming from the floor. Something was under the floorboards tapping at the wood, as if trying to find a way out. Fighting hysteria, Delilah managed to get her light on. As soon as the room was lit up, the tapping stopped.

Delilah was starting to get a little freaked out. She was so freaked out that she was now having trouble sleeping.

After her shift, Delilah was so exhausted, she'd fall into bed and go right to sleep. But then something would wake her at 1:35 a.m. Some sound or sensation, something just beyond the periphery of Delilah's consciousness, would intrude into her sleep and drag her into wakefulness.

Tonight, it was the sound of something in the wall between her apartment and Mary's.

It was a scratching sound, wasn't it? Or was it a droning? Could it have been an alarm? No, Delilah didn't think so. She was pretty sure something was moving around in the wall.

Delilah turned the light on and looked at her empty bedroom. She pulled her knees to her chest and tried to rein in her galloping heart.

Here was the problem with all these nocturnal intrusions: they all sounded like something trying to get to her, something sneaking up on her or beckoning to her in some way. Delilah was sure it was Ella.

The doll was still nearby. She had to be.

And she was functional. She just wasn't functional in a helpful way.

1:35 A.M.

Delilah had given this a lot of thought. A *ton* of thought. It was basically all she'd thought about for days.

She'd decided that Ella was not at all pleased about being tossed out. Maybe being discarded activated some subroutine that turned on new functions in Ella, hidden functions. Maybe the person who made Ella had a sick sense of humor and thought it would be a fun trick to play on someone who had the audacity to throw his creation away. Or maybe Ella malfunctioned.

Whatever. The bottom line was that Ella was out to get Delilah. Delilah could think of no other explanation for what was happening.

But what could she do about it?

She stared at the thin barrier between her domain and Mary's.

Mary.

What if Mary had the doll?

Mary's apartment looked out over the dumpsters, and she was home all day. What if she saw Delilah throw the doll away and she went out and got it?

Delilah had to find out.

Starting to get out of bed to go knock on Mary's door, Delilah stopped. It was the middle of the night. Pounding on someone's door in the middle of the night was a good way to start a confrontation. She didn't want a confrontation. She didn't want Mary to get defensive and hide Ella.

No. She'd have to wait until morning and try to get Mary to give up Ella by playing nice.

Mary was singing about penguins when Delilah got out of the shower at 7:30 a.m. Dressing in her exercise clothes because she figured she'd need a run after speaking to Mary, Delilah went into the kitchen and warmed up the slice of peach pie she'd brought back from the diner the night before. She didn't know much about Mary, but she did know Mary liked pie, especially peach pie.

Delilah left her apartment when Mary shifted into a verse about polar bears. As she knocked on Mary's flimsy front door, Mary belted out a line about an iceberg and then went silent. A second later, the door opened.

"Miss Delilah! What a nice surprise!" Mary grinned and reached out to grab Delilah.

Delilah barely had time to move the pie to the side before Mary's big arms pulled her into a tight hug. Delilah's nose got buried in Mary's substantial shoulder. Mary smelled like sausages and sweat and lavender.

"Hi, Mary," Delilah said when Mary released her.

She followed Mary into the peaceful Japan-inspired oasis that was Mary's apartment.

The first time Delilah had knocked on Mary's door to talk to her about the singing, Delilah had been expecting to find a cluttered apartment filled with knickknacks and books. Mary just looked like that kind of woman. About

1:35 A.M.

5'8" of well-padded, middle-aged frump, Mary had permed gray hair, a lined face, and round tortoise-shell glasses perched on a slightly upturned nose. She wore clothes in layers—vests over shirts over skirts over dresses, usually in a mismatched color hodgepodge.

But Mary's apartment looked nothing like Mary.

"Please take off your shoes," Mary sang when Delilah forgot.

"Oh right. Sorry." Delilah held the pie in one hand while she balanced on one foot and then the other to pull off her running shoes. She placed the shoes on the little rack just inside the door. Then she bowed to Mary when Mary bowed to her.

"I brought you peach pie." Delilah held out the warm pie container.

"Oh, that's just the thing!" Mary grabbed the container, bowed to Delilah again, and glided into her pristine kitchen to get chopsticks.

Delilah didn't know if Mary's decor and lifestyle came from a history with Japanese culture or whether Mary just fancied herself Japanese. She'd never asked because it felt rude to say, "What's with the Japanese stuff?"

But Delilah had read enough to know she was standing on a tatami mat and that a bamboo screen hid the bedroom door and that she was being ushered to blue-and-gray zabutons set up around a chabudai on the far side of the living room. A gnarled bonsai in a blue container sat on the chabudai. Other than the mat, the table, and the Japanese pillows, the living room was bare.

As Delilah sat on one of the gray cushions, she began questioning her idea that Mary had taken the doll. What would this strange woman want with a doll? It definitely didn't seem to suit her interior decor.

But then, Delilah had never seen Mary's bedroom. What if that door hid a collection of dolls in frilly dresses?

Mary placed a tea set on the chabudai, along with a plate of almond cookies, the pie container, and chopsticks. Having gone through the ritual before, Delilah let Mary pour the tea and offer her a cookie before she said anything. As Mary deftly scooped up a peach slice with her chopsticks, Delilah said, "I went to a cool garage sale the other day."

Mary placed the peach slice in her mouth, closed her eyes, and chewed with what looked like sheer joy. When she finished chewing, she leaned toward Delilah and waved a chopstick in front of Delilah's face.

"Secondhand stuff brings secondhand energy. Old hands. Bad hands. Tainted with story," Mary sang. She waved her chopstick back and forth like a metronome keeping time with her song's beat.

"You don't like secondhand things?"

Mary set down the chopsticks, grabbed the collar of her yellow blouse with both hands, and pulled the collar from her skin to shake it several times. She sang,

"Penguins, penguins, pull in the cold. Polar bears scare away the old."

Delilah frowned. She thought she'd figured out the secondhand song, but this new verse baffled her.

Mary let go of her collar and picked up her chopsticks again. "Hot flashes." She broke off a piece of crust and tweezed it between her chopsticks.

Delilah sipped tea and asked herself what she was doing here. How was she going to get an answer out of Mary? She'd be better off knocking out the woman and searching her apartment.

Delilah watched Mary eat. Even if she was capable of knocking someone out, which she wasn't, Delilah didn't think it would be a good idea to take on Mary. Mary was not only taller and bigger, she probably knew some kind of martial arts or something.

"The past leaves stains," Mary said.

"What?"

"No garage sales, no antique shops, no thrift stores. I don't want to open old doors," Mary intoned.

Delilah nodded. She was pretty sure she got that. If Mary didn't like old stuff because she thought old stuff had stains of the past, she wasn't likely to have pulled an old doll from a dumpster.

Not unless she had done it and now she was just messing with Delilah.

Delilah stared into Mary's eyes. Mary stopped eating pie and stared right back. Her eyes were pale green, streaked with swirls of yellow—kind of freaky. Delilah blinked and looked away. She stood.

"I need to go for a run," Delilah said.

"I need to finish my pie," Mary said.

"Okay. I'm sorry, but I have to go."

"No sorry, no sorry, no sorry. Just be, just be, just be," Mary sang.

"Okay. Uh, bye, Mary."

Of course, Mary's farewell was more singing: "Bye, bye, so long. Ta-ta, toodle-oo, until later, alligator."

Delilah waved at Mary and fled the woman's apartment.

On the tenth night of chilling 1:35 a.m. awakenings, Delilah knocked her lamp onto the floor in a pure panic to turn it on. Instead, she'd broken it, and she was whimpering in fear by the time she got her flashlight from the nightstand drawer and flipped its switch.

She was so sure the flashlight was going to reveal Ella at the side of her bed that she screamed as the light brightened the room.

But nothing was there.

Delilah, icy tendrils skittering all over her body, shot the flashlight beam all over the room. The light quivered as it scanned the darkness because Delilah's hand was shaking. With every new shift in the flashlight's direction, she absolutely expected the light to reveal Ella's face emerging out of the dim.

Where had the doll gone?

1:35 A.M.

Ella had been here. Delilah was sure of it.

What else could have made those soft little footfalls that snatched Delilah from her sleep? Delilah had been dreaming she was lying in a hammock, alone. Then she'd heard footsteps, small and light, pattering closer and closer. She'd awakened when they reached her.

Delilah kept shifting her flashlight's beam. And she listened. *There.* The soft steps. She aimed her light at her bedroom door. It was open.

Had she left it open?

She couldn't remember.

She thought she'd closed it, but she couldn't be sure.

She leaned toward the door and cocked her head, willing her ears to tell her what she was hearing. Were those footsteps in the living room?

She heard a click. Was that her front door?

Wanting to go look while also *not* wanting to go look, Delilah chose to give in to inertia. She stayed right where she was, clutching her flashlight with one hand and grasping her sheets close to her body with the other.

Still listening with every ounce of her being, she thought she heard a sound out in the hallway. Was that Mary's door opening and closing?

Delilah hesitated for another few seconds, then she jumped out of bed, ran to the wall, and turned on the light. She looked around her bedroom. Everything was normal.

She turned, opened the bedroom door the rest of

the way, and ran into the living room to turn on that light. Again, everything looked as it should have. Her apartment door was closed and bolted. She was alone.

That was the problem, wasn't it?

Delilah crossed to her love seat and pulled Harper's afghan around her shoulders. She sat sideways with her legs tucked under her.

By the time Delilah had met Harper, she'd resigned herself to being alone. Sure, she was surrounded by foster kids, but they weren't family, and they weren't friends, either . . . until Harper. None of them loved her, and she didn't love them. None of her foster parents had loved her, either.

No one loved Delilah until Harper came along. And even then, Harper couldn't love her enough.

After her parents died, Delilah didn't think she'd ever again be loved the way her parents had loved her . . . until she met Richard at a Halloween party. She was a senior in high school. He was a sophomore in college. Their gazes locked over eyeball-and-blood punch, and they spent the rest of the night dancing. When Richard decided to take a "sabbatical" from college, he begged Delilah, "the love of his life," to come along. She was just two weeks from turning eighteen, so they waited, and on her birthday, she said goodbye to Harper and the structure-happy Gerald. She headed off to Europe with Richard. It was January, so he took her to the Alps and taught her to ski.

For a year and a half, they played all over Europe. Finally, Richard's dad demanded that Richard come home and start working in the family business if he wasn't going to finish college. Richard proposed to Delilah. His parents and sister, with obvious reluctance, welcomed Delilah into the family. They had a fairy-tale wedding; Delilah had felt like a princess. Then they moved into his parents' guesthouse. From that point, all they had to do was stick to their plan. Richard would move up in the company. They'd have babies. They'd eventually get their own place. They were going to live happily ever after.

Instead, Delilah was here. Alone.

Or *not* alone.

She wasn't sure which was worse.

Every day, at 4:30 p.m., Mary left her apartment to go for her "daily constitutional." Even if Mary hadn't explained this to Delilah, she would have known because Mary sang about it.

Delilah had to get through two more workdays and two more terrifying 1:35 a.m. wake-ups before she had a day off so she was home at 4:30 p.m. Both of those nights, Delilah had listened to pit-a-pat and rat-a-tat sounds that convinced her Ella was retreating to Mary's apartment after she tormented Delilah. Delilah was convinced that Mary had Ella, no matter what Mary said about old stains. So she'd decided she was going to break into Mary's apartment and look for the doll.

This plan was only possible because working in a diner had some perks: you got to meet a large variety of people with a large variety of skills. One of Delilah's regulars was a private detective, Hank, and the night before, Delilah had asked him how hard it was to pick a lock.

"Depends on the lock," Hank had said, adjusting the vest of one of the three-piece suits he always wore.

"Simple apartment door lock," she'd said.

"Deadbolt?"

Delilah had shaken her head. Mary didn't use her deadbolt. She sang a lot about trust and faith.

Delilah had thought the detective would ask her why she wanted to know, but instead he just asked if any of the women in the place had a hairpin, and he'd taken one from Mrs. Jeffrey, an elderly woman who came in daily for rice pudding. He'd led Delilah to the door of the restaurant's storage room, and in five minutes, he'd taught her to pick a lock. Good thing Nate wasn't around. He wouldn't have liked knowing how easy it was to get into the supplies.

So thanks to Hank, it took Delilah only a minute to break into Mary's apartment. Once inside, she had to take another minute to get her breathing under control. Her heart felt like it was hopping around spastically like hot oil on a flat cooktop. Her legs felt weird, as if they were trying to run away while standing still.

Adrenaline, she thought.

1:35 A.M.

Clearly, she wasn't cut out to be a spy. She was a mess, and all she'd done was get inside the door.

"Well, why don't you get on with it so you can be done?" she asked herself.

She didn't think this was going to take long. Ella wasn't in the living room unless she was invisible. That left the kitchen cabinets, the bedroom, and the bathroom.

Delilah forced herself to move.

As she suspected, Mary's kitchen cabinets were sparsely filled and neatly organized. Ella was not hiding among the stoneware or inside Mary's wok. Nor was she in the refrigerator or the freezer.

The bathroom was similarly near empty. Just to be sure, Delilah checked the toilet tank. Not only was it empty of hidden items, it was unusually clean.

Delilah moved on to the bedroom. There, she met her first challenge.

Mary's bedroom was filled with storage bins—stacks and stacks of black plastic storage bins. They lined every wall, and a pairing of two each made up Mary's nightstands. Other than the storage bins, all that Mary's bedroom held was a futon and a pillow, both lying on the floor.

Delilah checked her watch. She had about forty minutes before Mary would be back. She wanted to be gone in thirty or less, to be safe. So she started opening bins.

Delilah discovered a lot about Mary in the next thirty-five minutes. She learned that Mary was at some point a teacher, that she was a widow, that she made or had once made beaded jewelry, that she loved musicals, that she had come from a family with three kids, and that she'd once had a child of her own who had died in a fire. Delilah figured that gave Mary the right to be a little weird. Mary had a laptop, which she apparently used to watch her movies, and she had an old manual typewriter. Mary typed up her songs. They filled seven of the fifty-three bins in the room.

Delilah, moving so fast she was dripping with sweat after the first eleven bins, looked in every bin. Ella was not in any of them.

Giving up and about to head for the door, Delilah backtracked and carefully poked the futon and the pillow. They were the only places left where Ella could be hiding. No Ella.

Delilah looked around to be sure she'd restacked all the bins neatly. She hoped she'd put them in the right order.

Even if she hadn't, she had to leave. Now. She'd gone well past her margin for safety.

She barely made it back to her apartment in time. Right after she closed and bolted her door, she heard Mary's singing voice trilling, "Blood flowing, heart pumping healthy, happy. Zing!"

Delilah leaned against her door, then slid to the floor. She was depleted and baffled. If Mary didn't have Ella, who did? And why wouldn't Ella leave her alone?

1:35 A.M.

* * *

On the thirteenth night of Delilah's sleep-invasion hell, Delilah heard an actual alarm at 1:35 a.m. It was so loud that she dreamed she was being attacked by a huge bee. She was running from the bee when she opened her eyes and reached for the lamp she'd bought at a garage sale. This lamp was metal with LED bulbs. It wouldn't break.

Delilah might, though.

The night before, Delilah had wondered, without much expectation at all, if she'd managed to live through the Twelve Nights of Ella. Maybe it would just stop. Because Delilah didn't know for sure why it had started, it could just stop. Right?

Wrong.

It wasn't stopping. In fact, now Delilah could still hear a buzzing in her ears, like a high-pitched whirring sound. Was she actually hearing that? Or was something wrong with her ears? What did tinnitus sound like? She'd heard about tinnitus from one of the old men who congregated in the diner daily to grouse about the state of their bodies and the state of the world in general. He'd said his ears rang all the time. Delilah wasn't hearing a ringing. It was a . . .

It was nothing. It had stopped.

Delilah turned over and put her face in her pillow. Why wouldn't Ella leave her alone? And where was she?

If Delilah could destroy Ella, it would stop. But she couldn't destroy what she couldn't find. The day after she searched Mary's place, Delilah had started wondering whether one of her other neighbors had gotten the doll out of the dumpster. She'd spent three hours knocking on every door in the building to ask if anyone had found Ella. Amazingly, only eight doors had gone unanswered. Everyone she spoke to had looked genuinely clueless about finding a doll. The next day and the next, she'd gotten to the rest of the building's inhabitants. She'd learned the eighth unanswered door belonged to an empty unit.

At 1:45 a.m. that next morning, she'd picked the lock to the empty apartment and checked for Ella there. No doll.

Delilah was beginning to have a problem that went beyond being awakened at 1:35 a.m. every night. The thing was that she wasn't just waking up every night at 1:35 a.m. She was being *terrorized* every night at 1:35 a.m. Every single night, some sound or smell or sensation stole into her sleep and wrestled her back into wakefulness. And now, for the first time in her life, she was having trouble sleeping at all. This problem had two prongs.

First, she was having trouble getting to sleep at the start of her night. Instead of feeling the stress ooze out of her body when she hit the bed, as it always had in the past, now when she lay down, her stress multiplied exponentially. As soon as her head touched the pillow, she had a sense of impending doom. It felt like her heart was bouncing around in her chest. She began sweating and trembling. Her throat got tight. She alternately felt frigid and then steaming hot. In spite of how fast her heart was beating, she couldn't catch her breath.

On the second night of this, which was the fifteenth night of the entire ordeal, Delilah called Harper. "I think I'm going to die," she told her friend.

"Talk to me," Harper said. "You have two minutes. I'm about to go on."

"Oh. Sorry."

"One minute, fifty-five seconds. Talk."

Delilah described what she was experiencing.

"You're having a panic attack. What's been going on lately?"

"You wouldn't believe me if I told you."

"Try me. But do it in a minute."

Delilah gave Harper the abbreviated version of her 1:35 a.m. torture.

"Why are you making such a big deal out of it? So you're waking up at the same time every night? Just go back to sleep."

"You don't understand."

"Apparently not. Try again tomorrow." Harper hung up. When the stage called, that was that.

Left on her own, again, Delilah looked up panic attacks on her computer. She discovered a variety of suggestions for dealing with them: deep breathing, muscle relaxation, deliberate focus, visualization of a happy place. Delilah focused on the first two, and she managed to fall asleep, only to be awakened at 1:35 a.m. by the sound of her deadbolt being thrown back. Launching herself from her bed, she bounded through her apartment to stop her intruder. But no one was intruding. Her deadbolt was secure. And her panic returned.

This brought her to the second prong of her sleep problem. Ella's nightly incursions into Delilah's sleep left Delilah feeling violated and petrified. She was literally quivering by the time whatever it was that woke her faded back into silence. She had to use the same deep breathing and muscle relaxation to get back to sleep. And they seemed to be losing effectiveness.

But still Delilah tried. Lying on her back now, she counted her breaths in and out. She was up to 254 before she started feeling even a little drowsy. Somewhere around 273, she finally went back to sleep.

"So you think this doll is ... what? Haunting you?" Harper asked. She sipped her espresso and flipped around her long, high ponytail, which went well with the fifties-style, full-skirted floral dress she had on today.

"No. Not *haunted*," Delilah said. "She's not a ghost. She's not possessed or whatever. She's technology. I think she's got defective programming."

"And she's what? Invisible? Got the keys to your

deadbolt? Able to walk through walls?" Harper threw up her hands, and the multitude of bracelets around her thin wrists jangled. "I mean, there's technology and then there's magic. What you're talking about goes a little beyond technology, don't you think? Especially for an old doll."

Delilah frowned and shook her head. It infuriated her that Harper was bringing up the very points that Delilah was hung up on herself. Her theory didn't make sense. But what other theory was there?

"Have you looked into the meaning of the number itself?" Harper asked. She looked over at the counter and winked at a cute guy ordering a latte. Returning her attention to Delilah, she said, "Maybe your subconscious is trying to tell you something."

"You mean like the 333 thing?"

Harper shrugged. "Every number has a meaning, a resonance."

"Uh-huh."

For as long as Delilah had known Harper, she'd been a little out there. "I'm a right-brained free spirit," Harper said the first time Delilah had laughed at one of Harper's spiritual flights of fancy. "Deal with it."

"I'm not kidding. Let's see." Harper pulled her phone from her pocket and tapped it a few times. "Okay. Here it is. Oh hey, this is interesting." She looked up.

"I don't care," Delilah said. "I don't want to know. I don't believe in that stuff anyway."

Harper shrugged. "Whatever. It's your funeral."

★ ★ ★

That night, deep breathing didn't help Delilah get to sleep. After an hour of lying in her bed, exhausted but still too panicked to sleep, she sat up, grabbed her pillow and her comforter, and went out to the living room. There, she curled up on the sofa, tucked the comforter around her, and was asleep in just a few more deep breaths.

She was asleep until something started crawling on the ceiling above her.

Delilah's eyes sprang open. She clawed for her flashlight, pushed the button, and aimed it at the ceiling. Delilah fully expected to see Ella clinging to the ceiling over her head; she could even hear fingernails rasping against drywall.

But nothing was there. Nothing at all. Delilah shined the flashlight around all over the ceiling. And she listened.

Stiffening, she pointed her light at the corner of the ceiling, where it sounded like something was scrabbling toward the wall. Delilah squinted, as if doing so would help her see through the opaque structures of her apartment. Of course, squinting didn't help.

And neither did sleeping on the sofa.

The sofa didn't keep Ella from tugging Delilah from sleep at 1:35 a.m. the next night, either, but it did seem to help Delilah get back to sleep. It was only after the strange snicking sound retreated into the kitchen that

1:35 A.M.

Delilah was able to slow her breathing enough to find sleep again.

The next night, though, the sofa had nothing to offer her. First, it took her just as long to get to sleep on the sofa as it had been taking in her bed. Second, the sofa couldn't soothe her after she felt a light touch on her shoulder at 1:35 a.m.

This time Delilah was awakened, she didn't have to turn on a light when she woke up. She'd never turned the lights out. The fact that Delilah didn't see Ella as soon as Delilah opened her eyes gave Delilah a clue about just how advanced her nemesis was. Ella could disappear in the blink—or the opening—of an eye.

Delilah knew Ella had disappeared that fast because the doll *had* been there. She had to have been there. Something touched Delilah. The touch had been baby soft. Ella soft. Little fingers. Just a hint of a brush against Delilah's nightshirt-covered shoulder. No more than a hint of contact. But it had been enough to turn Delilah's intestines into a tangled mass of fear and transform her blood into liquid nitrogen. She felt like she was being frozen and broken apart from within.

Delilah stood, clenching her comforter and her pillow. She couldn't stay out here in the living room.

She looked around like a gazelle searching for a place the lion couldn't reach. Her gaze landed on the bathroom door. She ran for the little room and dove, with her comforter and pillow, into the bathtub. Curling into the tightest ball she could manage, she pulled the comforter over her head.

The next night, Delilah started in the bathtub. And still, Ella found her. At 1:35 a.m., Delilah heard something creeping through the pipes under the tub. Sure Ella's hand was going to burst through the porcelain and grab her, Delilah had scrambled out of the tub and into the corner of the bathroom, against the door, where she spent the next four hours trying to breathe. She didn't even attempt sleep.

At 5:35 a.m., Delilah got dressed and went over to the diner. Nate, as she knew he would be, was baking biscuits and cinnamon rolls.

"What're you doing here?" he asked when she stepped into the kitchen. "I thought putting you on the same shift all the time had eliminated your time confusion. Now you're showing up for shifts you're not on instead of being late for ones you are on." Nate chopped biscuit dough into neat squares and began throwing them into perfectly straight lines on a massive baking sheet.

The diner smelled gloriously ordinary. Coffee aromas mingled with the scents of buttermilk and cinnamon. The sounds were comfortingly normal, too. A couple of their early regulars were discussing the weather at the counter. One of the servers was whistling. The walk-in refrigerator hummed.

1:35 A.M.

"I need you to put me on nights," Delilah said to Nate.

Nate stopped in mid-throw. He turned and raised both eyebrows. "You messing with me?"

Delilah shook her head. "I'm having trouble sleeping at night. It's . . . well, it's a thing. I figure if I work nights, I can sleep during the day. I know Grace hates managing the night shift. She'd be happy to trade with me, I'm sure."

"You're a better manager. I like having you here when it's busy."

"Thanks."

"That wasn't a compliment. It was a statement of fact and a complaint."

"You're just a teddy bear under all that bluster," Delilah said.

It was true. Nate complained about every employee and every customer and the diner in general, and he loved them all.

"You tell anyone, and I'll have to kill you."

Delilah mimed zipping her mouth shut.

Nate sighed. "Okay. Switch. But do what you can to work out the 'thing.'"

"Thanks."

"Be here at ten. And *do not* be late."

"I'm going to buy two new alarm clocks right now."

"Good girl."

★ ★ ★

Delilah didn't know why she didn't think of it before. How could Ella plague Delilah at 1:35 a.m. if Delilah was already awake at that time? There was no way Ella could sneak up on Delilah at the restaurant. So all Delilah had to do was work nights until Ella ran out of juice or whatever. Problem solved.

Even though Delilah had never liked the night shift when she'd worked it before, she was so buoyed by her plan to be free of Ella that she went to work in the best mood she'd been in for a long time. She was so upbeat when she clocked in at 9:55 p.m. that Glen, the night-shift cook, asked her if she was all right.

"Freedom, Glen," she said. "This is what freedom looks like."

"Weird is what you look like," he said. But he grinned to let her know he didn't hold it against her.

Glen was a huge guy with a gut that sometimes caught fire when he hung it over the grill. In spite of his size, he was energetic. She thought he was pretty young, maybe in his late twenties. He had a baby face, chin-length sideburns, and kind brown eyes. She liked working with him.

For three hours and thirty-nine minutes, Delilah felt great. She chatted with all the late-night regulars, letting a couple of the old guys flirt with her. She didn't even mind the couples, the ones who came in after late shows, the ones who used to make her feel desperately alone.

1:35 A.M.

At 1:34 a.m., Delilah stepped into the walk-in refrigerator to grab some cheese and some lettuce. For some reason, salads were popular tonight.

She was just bending over to reach for the cheddar when she heard an alarm going off in the kitchen. Rising up, she whacked her head on the shelf above her. She ignored the pain and looked at her watch. It was 1:35 a.m.

Tearing out of the walk-in, Delilah spun in a circle in the kitchen. "Where's that coming from?" she shouted.

Glen looked up from the grill. Jackie, the night server, dropped a plate and stared at Delilah with wide blue eyes.

"Where's what coming from?" Glen asked.

"That!"

The alarm was similar to the torture device that Gerald had used. It had that same ringing, buzzing, shrieking undulation.

Delilah ran to the deep fryer and looked at its controls. No, it wasn't going off. She checked the ovens. They weren't even being used. She tore into the employee break room. No, the sound wasn't coming from in there. It was out in the kitchen. Delilah returned to the middle of the stainless-steel maze and began searching through pots, pans, and utensils. She didn't do it neatly or methodically, and when she tossed her third pan, Glen grabbed her arm.

"Hey, Lady Delilah, you trippin'?"

"What?" Delilah wrested her arm from Glen's grasp. "No. Don't you hear—?"

The sound stopped. Delilah tilted her head and listened but all she could hear now were the normal diner noises.

She looked at Glen and at Jackie, who was still staring like Delilah had just turned into an elephant. "You two didn't hear that?" she asked.

"Heard you shouting and throwing pans around," Glen said.

Delilah looked at Jackie. A year or two younger than Delilah and still unsure of herself, Jackie wore bright blue glasses; the lenses made her eyes look huge with shock.

Jackie shook her head. "I didn't hear anything. I mean, um, other than, um, you, and the usual, um, stuff."

This couldn't be happening.

How could Ella have followed Delilah over here?

Well, why *couldn't* she follow Delilah over here? Hadn't Ella already demonstrated she could do pretty much whatever she wanted?

Which was crazy. This was just technology gone awry. Right?

"You gonna be okay?" Glen asked.

Delilah shook her head. "Yeah."

And she figured she would be. At least she didn't have to try to go to sleep with her heart pounding so loudly she was sure Glen and Jackie could hear it and were just being too polite to say so.

So her plan hadn't worked, but the upside was she could use her adrenaline-driven energy surge for work instead of trying to fight it so she could go to sleep. And maybe tomorrow night, because she was prepared for the alarm sound now, she could ignore it and get on with her shift. Maybe her new plan would work after all.

On the second night shift, Delilah made sure she wasn't alone at 1:35 a.m. She stuck close to Glen, which he didn't seem to mind. But in spite of being with him, she still lost it.

She couldn't help it. Tonight, for the first time, she hadn't just heard or sensed something. She'd *seen* something. She'd seen a flash of bright blue in the walk-in when Jackie opened the door. When she saw what she was sure was Ella coming out of the walk-in, Delilah screamed and pressed against Glen. He didn't seem to mind that, either, but he did ask why she was screaming. She had no answer for him.

At 1:30 a.m. the third night of Delilah's switch to night shift, Delilah was behind the counter. She'd decided the way to make sure nothing spooked her tonight was to stay out here in the open, well away from the walk-in.

When Mrs. Jeffrey, the rice pudding regular, came into the diner, Delilah was thrilled. She could serve Mrs. Jeffrey and 1:35 a.m. would just go on by.

"Hi, Delilah." Mrs. Jeffrey took a seat on one of the swiveling padded counter stools. Her eyes were puffy.

Delilah leaned on the counter. "Hi, Mrs. Jeffrey. Having trouble sleeping?"

Mrs. Jeffrey patted her tousled hair. "I suppose it's obvious. I do hope you still have some rice pudding left."

"Absolutely. I'll just—"

Delilah stopped. She looked over her shoulder. Then she glanced at the clock. It was 1:33 a.m.

Where was Jackie?

No way did Delilah want to go back into the walk-in. She was sure Ella would be in there waiting for her.

"Jackie?" she called.

No answer.

"Jackie!" It came out as a bellow.

Glen stuck his head out of the kitchen.

"Is there a problem?"

Delilah tried to calm her breathing. She was building up to a full-blown anxiety attack, and she didn't want to have one of those in front of her customer and coworkers.

Delilah looked at Mrs. Jeffrey. The elderly woman's brown eyes were wide.

"Sorry," Delilah said. "It's just . . ."

She stopped when the counter stool next to Mrs. Jeffrey started spinning back and forth. She blinked and she realized Ella was on the stool.

Ella was playing on the stool!

"Stop it!" Delilah clambered over the counter and grabbed the stool.

That's when Jackie entered the dining room. Delilah glanced at Jackie, and she realized she was sprawled over the counter, her butt up in the air. No wonder Jackie was gawking at her, openmouthed.

"Are you all right, dear?" Mrs. Jeffrey asked.

Delilah slid off the counter. "You didn't see the doll on the stool?"

"Doll? That's my purse, dear." Mrs. Jeffrey patted a bright blue purse, which sat on the stool next to her.

Delilah backed away from the counter. She checked the clock. Of course it was 1:35 a.m.

The next night something similar happened. Delilah stayed in the dining room, but she was still traumatized at 1:35 a.m. when she saw something moving around in the trash bin under the counter. Wanting to believe it was a mouse, even though that would have been horrible for the diner, she'd used a fork to search the rubbish. She didn't find a mouse. But she spotted a pink ruffle that made her drop the fork and jump back. She'd resisted the urge to scream, but she hadn't been able to resist the urge to hurl the trash bin out the back door of the diner, scattering trash but no Ella—who, as usual, had instantly moved on—all over the pavement.

Delilah just couldn't contain her reactions. She knew

Glen and Jackie were watching her, but that wasn't enough to keep her calm.

It was the fifth night of night shift that did Delilah in.

Even though it hadn't worked so well yet, Delilah still thought the safest place for her in the diner was the main dining room. She did her best to avoid closed-in places like the walk-in, the supply room, and Nate's office.

At 1:30 a.m. on the fifth night, the diner was empty of customers. Delilah and Jackie were filling the small glass salt and pepper containers. Delilah had salt; Jackie had pepper. They had the tray of containers set up at a table by the diner's front window, and they sat on opposite sides of the table. While they worked, Jackie chattered about her college classes. Delilah tried to pay attention, but she was mentally counting down the minutes and seconds to 1:35 a.m.

What was it going to be tonight?

Every muscle and joint in Delilah's body was stiff with dread.

But when Delilah spotted something bright blue flutter through the parking lot in front of the diner, her muscles and joints released and went into action. She jumped up, knocking the tray of salt and pepper shakers onto the floor with a loud crash, and she sprinted out the diner's front door. Rushing through the nearly empty parking lot, she scanned for Ella's dress.

She was sure that was what she'd seen. She'd seen

the trailing edge of Ella's fluffy dress. The doll was out here. She'd been watching Delilah.

When she didn't see Ella, Delilah started looking under the two parked cars at the edge of the lot. She was bending to check under the first one when someone grabbed her shoulder.

She screamed.

"Okay. Okay. You're okay." It was Glen. His face looked pale in the mottled light.

"Did you see her?" Delilah asked.

"See who?"

She looked into Glen's eyes. He was so sympathetic and concerned.

Delilah crumpled into Glen's arms and started to cry.

Delilah thought it was pretty amazing that she'd gotten through twenty-three nights of 1:35 a.m. horror without crying. In fact, she hadn't even noticed that she didn't cry.

But once she started crying, she couldn't stop. She cried so much that after Glen got her inside, he called Nate and asked him to come in. Nate arrived as Jackie was sweeping up broken glass from the diner floor. While Delilah sat in a back booth and tried to get her body to stop twitching, Nate talked to Glen and Jackie. She couldn't hear what they said, but she figured she should say something on her own behalf. She stood.

"Come with me," Nate said.

Good. He was taking her to his office. She could explain things there.

Or not. As soon as they entered his office, Nate closed the door behind him. "I'm sorry, Delilah. I have to let you go."

Delilah looked at Nate with wide eyes that felt bruised and lacerated.

"Don't look at me like that." Nate went around his desk and dropped into his leather chair.

Delilah twisted her mouth and tried not to whimper.

"I've cut you all kinds of slack for being late. I've worked around your 'thing,' but this is too much. Jackie says you've been acting 'super weird'"—he gave the words air quotes—"the last four nights. And now this. I can't keep an employee who freaks out the customers and breaks trays full of salt and pepper shakers."

"Nate, I—"

"Don't. Don't even try to give me a sob story. I'm not your father. Whatever you have going on that made you do what you did tonight is something you need to work out on your own, outside this diner. You're a good worker when you're here and focused, but I can't afford the liability risks of you acting like this." He rubbed his beard. "I'll have someone bring you your last check tomorrow."

Delilah stood in front of Nate's scarred old desk and looked at all its neat little piles. She turned. She wasn't going to beg for the job.

1:35 A.M.

As she left the diner, she wasn't even thinking about the job. She was thinking about Ella.

Every night was getting worse. How was she going to get through another 1:35 a.m.?

When Richard had asked Delilah to move out of his parents' guesthouse, she'd had no place to go, so she'd gone to Harper. Harper welcomed her with open arms, but unfortunately, Harper lived in a house with ten other struggling actors. All Harper had to offer was half of a double bed–size mattress on the floor of what once was a massive walk-in closet (massive for a closet, not so much for a place to sleep). Harper loved her "retreat." She got the bed, and she got to organize all her clothes on the racks and shelves of the closet. Delilah hated the tiny space. It gave her claustrophobia. Plus, Harper snored and talked in her sleep. Delilah had only stayed with Harper three days before getting her apartment with the money Richard had given her.

So it said a lot about her state of mind that she called Harper when she got home from work and asked if she could stay with Harper for a few nights.

"Sure thing," Harper said. "We'll have a slumber party. You won't even know 1:35 a.m. has come and gone."

Delilah wanted to believe that was true. She tried to believe it.

Harper was performing that evening, as she did six evenings a week, so she left Delilah in the care of one of her housemates, a funky guy named Rudolph, who spent the afternoon and evening teaching Delilah the card game he'd created. She never did fully understand it, but she had to admit it was entertaining. Rudolph was funny and nice, too.

By the time Harper got home about 12:30 a.m., Delilah was surprisingly relaxed.

"Okay," Harper said, dragging Delilah away from a disappointed Rudolph. "You don't get to keep her as a pet, Rudy," she chastised.

He stuck out his lower lip, then grinned at Delilah as Delilah followed Harper to the second floor of the house.

"I have munchies," Harper said. "The salty kind. Guaranteed to keep away snarky high-tech dolls."

Delilah's stomach did a somersault at the word *doll*.

Harper led Delilah into her "bedroom," threw several bags and boxes of chips and crackers on the mattress, and then said, "I need to go wash off the face paint. Be right back."

Delilah sat on the mattress, opened a box of cheese crackers, and nibbled on one. Her stomach continued to do gymnastics.

When Harper returned, she entertained Delilah with stories about that evening's performance. "So first, Manny forgot his line, and then he said *my* line," Harper said as she tore into a bag of barbecue potato chips. "Imbecile. I had to think fast. So I kissed him."

"Was that in character?"

"My character's a bit of a doodlebug. So pretty much anything is in character."

Delilah looked at her watch. It was 12:55 a.m.

"Hey, did you just look at your watch?" Harper grabbed Delilah's arm. "Gimme that."

Delilah didn't resist when Harper took off Delilah's watch and stuffed it under a pillow. She didn't need it anyway. She'd know when 1:35 a.m. came.

"No watch. No 1:35 a.m." Harper wiped her hands in a "that's that" gesture.

Delilah wanted it to be that easy.

But it wasn't. She knew exactly when 1:35 a.m. rolled around. She knew because suddenly, a voice said, "It's time."

Delilah jumped up and hit her head on the rack above the bed.

"What're you doing?" Harper asked at the same time Delilah ducked her head under the rack and said, "Did you do that?"

Then they both spoke at the same time again. "What do you mean?" Delilah said. "Do what?" Harper said.

They both stopped. Delilah could still hear Gerald's voice in her ear repeating, "It's time" in a receding echo.

Delilah looked down at Harper. "Do you hear that?"

Harper frowned up at Delilah. "I don't hear anything except Raul's oldies music and the movie Kate and Julia are watching downstairs."

"You didn't just mimic Gerald?"

"I'm sitting right here in front of you. I'm eating potato chips. How could I have mimicked Gerald?" Harper popped a chip into her mouth with deliberate emphasis. She chewed loudly.

Delilah shook her head. She realized she was shivering. She had to clench her teeth together to keep them from chattering.

"Then you must have Ella."

"What?"

Delilah's neck was starting to hurt from her contorted position under the closet rack. And her legs felt weak. She sank onto the bed.

"You know what Gerald sounds like."

"So?"

"So you could program Ella to sound like him, record yourself mimicking him or something."

Harper shoved aside the chips bag and leaned toward Delilah. "I want to be sure I'm understanding what you're saying." She narrowed her eyes. "You're saying I took your wacky doll and somehow got her to work, and I recorded my impression of Gerald on the doll so it could play that for you. That's what you're saying?"

Delilah shook her head.

"No?" Harper asked. "Then what are you saying?"

"That is what I'm saying. I'm just—"

"You're just crazy is what you're just. I don't have the stupid doll. I never saw the stupid doll. If I had *seen* the doll

1:35 A.M.

and had *taken* the doll, I sure wouldn't have recorded something on it to scare you. Why would I do that?"

"I don't know." Delilah looked at her hands. She felt a little stupid. Why would Harper do that?

Then she remembered the voice she heard. But who else could have done it?

"You tell me," Delilah said. "Why did you do it?"

"I didn't do it!" Harper shouted.

Delilah flinched. Then she whispered, "But there's no other explanation."

Harper stared at Delilah. "Jeez. Del. You're losing it, girl." She shoved the junk food off the bed and curled up on her side with her back to Delilah. "I'm going to sleep."

"I wish I could."

"You could," Harper said. "Just get out of your head."

"It's not me. It's Ella."

Harper sighed, then started breathing deeply and evenly.

"Must be nice," Delilah muttered.

The next day, Delilah spent most of the day hanging out with Harper and her housemates. Because she didn't fall asleep until almost 7:00 a.m. and Harper woke her when she got up at about 10 a.m., Delilah was fuzzy with sleep deprivation. She felt like someone had stuffed her brain with cotton candy.

When she got up, Harper seemed either to have forgotten Delilah's accusations or forgiven them. She didn't say anything about what had happened between them, and she was her usual vivacious self all day. Delilah decided not to say anything else about Ella. She also decided, though, that she wasn't staying here tonight. She'd leave while Harper was at the theater.

She didn't know until she walked out to her car at 4:35 p.m. where she was going to go. It came to her in a flash of brilliant insight. She'd go to a motel, a motel on the other side of town. Ella wouldn't be able to find her there. Delilah didn't think anyone else, like Harper, would find her there, either. She wasn't going to use an assumed name or anything, but Harper didn't process things in the sort of organized way that she'd think to do a search of motels and find out if her friend was staying there.

So at 6:15 p.m., after Delilah ate a burger and fries at a fast-food place, she checked into the Bed4U Motel on the outskirts of the scruffier side of town. The quality level of the hotel was evident in both its name and the fact that its fading sign announced "A bed and a TV in every room."

"Talk about luxury," Delilah said when she parked her car over weeds growing through cracks in the time-worn asphalt.

The price was right, though. Trying not to breathe in smells of bleach and stewed cabbage in the hotel's small, brown lobby, Delilah paid for three nights. She was happy that the total barely made a dent in the credit

1:35 A.M.

limit on her one credit card. She was also happy that she got a room at the far end of the long, low building in the back, away from the traffic. The heavy woman behind the desk wasn't interested in Delilah at all. She was too busy watching a documentary about spiders on an old TV mounted on the wall next to the check-in counter.

The old hotel room was surprisingly neat and clean. Done in the same ugly brown tones Delilah had found in the lobby, the room wouldn't win any beauty prizes, but it smelled fresh, and everything worked. The bed was even comfortable.

Because the only other surfaces in the room suitable for sitting were a couple of straight-backed cloth-covered chairs, Delilah plopped on the bed as soon as she bolted the door and set her stuff on the low bureau across from the bed. She was pleased to discover the motel was pretty well insulated. The traffic on the busy road in front of the motel was just a distant *shhh*, and Delilah couldn't hear anything else. She'd thought she might watch some TV when she got in the room, but she was so tired she risked lying back on the pillow. Tense, expecting the usual panic attack symptoms, she was thrilled when she felt nothing but exhaustion.

She closed her eyes.

And sleep took her from the motel room into the promise . . . or portent . . . of her dreams.

★ ★ ★

The sound crept through her sleep like a spider crawling through her synapses and leaving silken trails along her neuropathways. It was a scuffing sound, like something scooting over a rough surface.

Her mind couldn't make enough sense of it to integrate it into her dream about riding horses. So the horse in her dream threw her off, and she came face-to-face with the spider.

She screamed. And the scream slung her back into consciousness.

Delilah's eyes opened, and she realized she was still screaming. She pressed her lips together and bit her tongue. She wanted to get up and run, but she couldn't. She was paralyzed.

Wait. Was she awake?

She thought she was.

Above her something crawled on the roof. It made a similar sound to the one in her dream, but this sound was worse. It wasn't just the sound of some spider going about its business. This was a strategic sound. It started. It stopped. It moved here. It moved there. It was a searching sound, a seeking sound. It was the sound of something with an objective.

And Delilah knew *she* was the objective.

Ella had found Delilah. She was looking for a way into the motel room.

Whining like a kitten being hunted by a coyote, Delilah struggled to free her limbs from whatever force held her

1:35 A.M.

immobile. But she was still pinned to the bed. The only thing she could do was move her head. So she turned her head and looked at the digital clock on the bedside table. It read, of course, 1:35 a.m.

As soon as Delilah saw the time, she discovered she could move. She thrashed free of the bedspread, which she'd managed to wrap around herself in her sleep. She jumped from the bed and crouched against the wall by the door, her gaze riveted on the ceiling.

Flashing dark-red light from a neon sign next door to the motel splayed across the ceiling like blood spatter. It was sporadically illuminated by the flickering fluorescent lamps that lit up the motel walkways and parking lot.

This meant Delilah could see what she needed to see. Nothing was coming through the ceiling. But that didn't comfort her. Ella had other ways to get into the room. And even if she didn't get into the room, the very fact that she was outside the room, on the roof, meant that Delilah's brief respite was over.

There was no getting away from Ella.

Delilah began rocking back and forth like a child. And she hummed until daylight broke. She didn't know what she was humming at first, but then she recognized the tune. She was humming the old lullaby her mom used to sing to her when she was little.

Even though Delilah had paid for three nights, she left the motel room about noon the next day. There was no point in staying. She couldn't sleep. She wasn't safe there.

She was pretty sure she wasn't safe anywhere, but Delilah figured being mobile wasn't a bad idea. This assumed, though, that Ella's circuits hadn't noted the make, model, color, and maybe even the license plate of Delilah's car. Ella had, after all, ridden to the apartment in the car. She probably had left some sort of tracker in it. Delilah's travels were no doubt a pointless waste of time and gasoline.

But what else could Delilah do?

So she drove.

She drove all afternoon and all evening. She drove all over the city, exploring neighborhoods she hadn't known existed. She gazed longingly at big family homes and children playing in the park. She cruised the shopping district, remembering what it was like to be able to buy whatever she wanted, and also remembering how little pleasure that had given her. She'd never wanted things. She'd wanted love.

When the sun started going down a little after six, Delilah realized she was being stupid. Very stupid. Why was she staying in the city? Why not get out of town, drive out into the country. Wouldn't it be harder for Ella to reach her there?

Delilah turned at a busy corner and pointed her car toward the freeway.

Then she immediately turned again, looping back into the neighborhood she'd just left.

1:35 A.M.

Maybe she wasn't being stupid after all. What if the city was helping to keep her safe? What if Ella would be free to do whatever she wanted to do to Delilah if they were away from a populated area?

Besides, in the country, it was dark. Very dark. Delilah had only one small flashlight. She didn't think she could stand facing 1:35 a.m. in the pitch dark. No. She'd stay in town.

But where?

Pulling into the drive-through of a fast-food burrito place, Delilah bought a chicken-and-rice burrito with sour cream. Weirdly, even though she was so scared she was probably just one more shock from full-blown hysteria, she still had her appetite. Maybe her body knew she needed nutrition to handle what was coming her way.

Delilah ate her burrito at a drive-in movie theater she discovered on the west edge of the city. She'd had no idea it was there. She was happy to find it, though. It kept her awake until nearly midnight. That's when the last movie—a chase-scene-heavy action flick—ended, and Delilah had to join the ragged line of cars straggling out of the drive-in. That's when she had to decide where she should be when 1:35 a.m. came around.

She'd thought about parking her car behind a dark building or in a quiet neighborhood near an unoccupied house. But did she really want to make it that easy for Ella to get to her?

No. It would be better if she was driving around at 1:35 a.m. She'd never tried that before. Maybe that was the trick.

So as her limbs got more jittery, and her breath came faster, and her lungs got tighter, Delilah drove closer and closer to the city center. She wanted to be where people still meandered down the sidewalks and bright lights turned night into day.

At 1:33 a.m., Delilah had an even more inspired idea. She'd drive onto one of the big bridges. Surely Ella couldn't get to her there, especially since the decision to hit the on-ramp to the bridge was as spontaneous as you could get.

Even though it was the middle of the night, at least a dozen cars were on the bridge. Delilah's hands sweated, and she repositioned them on the steering wheel. She blinked several times to clear her vision, which was becoming blurry. She concentrated on the road and forced herself not to look at her dashboard digital clock.

But she knew when 1:35 a.m. arrived.

She knew because that's when she heard her passenger door unlock and unlatch. Gasping and losing control of the car for an instant, Delilah turned the wheel to get back in her lane. The whooshing sound of wind coming through the open passenger door hit her just before she heard the passenger door slam closed again. She glanced to her right, her whole body charged with terror. She fully expected to see Ella sitting in the car next to her.

1:35 A.M.

But nothing was there.

All she saw in her car was a bag of fast-food trash, her purse, and her flashlight.

Almost across the bridge, she put her gaze back on the road. Then something hit the roof of her car with a *thunk*.

Delilah screamed and jammed her foot onto the accelerator. Her car scooted forward, and she pulled out to pass a minivan, barely missing its back bumper. She then jerked her car back into the right lane so she could take the first exit off the bridge.

Driving like a madwoman, Delilah careened onto the industrial road running parallel to the river and pulled over when she reached a boarded-up factory. Her car skidded to a stop, spraying gravel.

Delilah had the engine off and was out of the car the minute the vehicle stopped moving. She didn't bother to lock it up. She just grabbed her purse and her flashlight, slammed the driver's door behind her, and ran.

She ran toward the river, behind the factory. Her feet crackling over crumbling concrete and trash, she ran until she was hidden from the road. Her car was no longer in sight, either.

Delilah could still see where she was going because the factory, though empty, was well lit. She stopped running and looked around.

She had no idea where she was, but she didn't feel safe. Where would she ever feel safe again?

Turning in a full circle, she scanned her surroundings.

Maybe if she could hide from Ella now, the doll wouldn't find her later.

But where could she hide?

Delilah spotted a drainage pipe at the far side of the factory. It was huge, maybe four feet in diameter. She could crawl into that easily.

Striding across a dirt and gravel lot filled with potholes, Delilah headed toward the drainage pipe. But halfway there, she stopped. She couldn't take her purse with her. She couldn't take anything with her. She didn't know what linked her to Ella.

Turning in another circle, Delilah saw a stack of railroad ties. That should work. She checked her surroundings again. She was still alone. She ran over to the railroad ties and hid her purse in a crevice. Then she looked around once more and bolted over to the drainage pipe. She crawled inside and hunkered down. She realized she was light-headed. She was hyperventilating.

Leaning over, her head between her knees, she attempted to shorten her breaths, taking in less oxygen than she was sure she needed. She wished she had a paper bag. There was one in the car, but she couldn't go back there.

She couldn't go back to anyplace she'd ever been before. She couldn't go back to her life.

Ella was going to find her anywhere.

Even here.

Delilah fell back onto her butt and curled up in a ball,

hugging her legs close. She tried to stay silent, but she couldn't. She began to keen.

The sound that came from her wasn't like any sound she'd made before.

Not even when her parents died.

Not even when her first foster home refused to keep her.

Not even when her fourth foster dad beat her.

Not even when Gerald scheduled when she could blow her nose.

Not even when Richard threw her out.

The sound contained every hurt and fear and crushing disappointment she'd ever had—all rolled into one screeching rejection of pain. The sound she made was the sound of a woman who had no strength left. She couldn't fight anymore.

Delilah closed her mouth. Her throat hurt. Her lungs hurt. Her heart hurt.

And she couldn't stop quaking. Her whole body was almost convulsing with apprehension.

No, not apprehension.

Delilah was so far beyond any known version of fear that she didn't feel human anymore.

She was never going to be safe again.

Delilah sobbed as she got onto her hands and knees. She couldn't stay here. Ella would know where she was.

Crawling as fast as she could, her hands stinging from the rough concrete surface chafing at her skin, Delilah clambered out of the drainage pipe. She stood.

Where could she go?

Delilah began to run again. She ran parallel to the river, scanning this way and that, looking for a way out, looking for an escape hatch, an ejection seat, something to take her as far from Ella as she could get.

She didn't know how long she ran before she stumbled into what looked like an abandoned construction site. Its lumpy outlines were shrouded by the darkness, but street lamps sent enough light over it to reveal its basic outlines. She slowed her pace, aimed her flashlight, and studied the weathered sign announcing the project. It looked like an office complex.

Shoving at a dirty board covering an opening in the side of what seemed to be a three-story structure, Delilah sidled into the site. The answer to her plight was in here. She was sure of it.

Someplace here, she was going to find a way to escape Ella forever. But where?

Picking her way over bare boards sprinkled with nails and screws, weaving around stacks of lumber and drywall, Delilah made her way into a room that was nearly completed. The drywall wasn't just up; it was also textured and painted. And there, high up on the inside wall, was her answer.

It was a vent opening, uncovered, barely big enough for her to slip into. That was the way. That was where she could stop running from Ella.

Looking around the room for a way to boost herself up

to the opening, she spotted an overturned sawhorse. She trotted over to it, righted it, and carried it to a spot below the vent. It was strong and stable.

Stopping to listen, to be sure she was alone, Delilah hoisted herself onto the sawhorse, stood on her tiptoes, and was able to hook her hands over the front of the vent opening. From there, she did a pull-up, thankful for all the upper-body strength she got from heavy cleaning at the diner.

Once her head was level with the vent opening, she reached in with one arm, searching for some kind of handhold. She didn't find one, but her sweaty hand stuck to the metal enough to give her some purchase. She was able to wiggle her upper body into the vent opening by going one hand length at a time. Once she was that far into the vent, she just had to wiggle her whole body, like a snake, into the vent.

But she still didn't feel safe.

She stopped wriggling for a moment, taking stock. Turning on her flashlight, she spotted a downward turn in the vent. She inched toward it.

Yes. This was it.

Aiming her head down into the chute-like space, she scooted forward.

A little farther.

And a little farther.

Her flashlight slipped from her sweaty hand and clinked against the metal vent walls as it dropped out of

Delilah's reach. She heard it impact something with a sharp crack. It must have broken because the space went dark.

Delilah's shoulders wedged her so tightly into the compact metal enclosure that she knew she'd finally found it. This was where Ella couldn't find her.

No one would find her here.

Trying to move just to be sure, she confirmed that she was stuck, completely and thoroughly stuck.

Her breathing slowed. She relaxed.

She couldn't move in any direction.

She'd never have to run from Ella again.

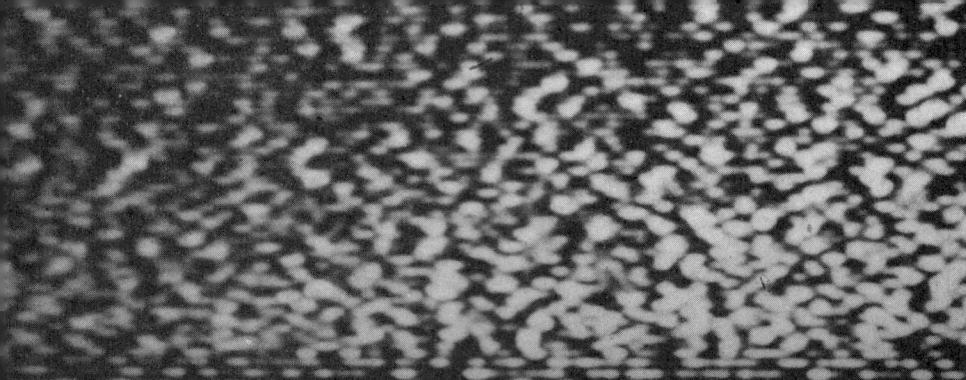

ROOM FOR ONE MORE

To tell the truth, Stanley didn't like the place. Something about the way it was hidden from passersby made him wonder what secrets were being kept there. Was it even a legitimate business, or were sketchy deals being made under the table? Stanley didn't know. When he was hired, the supervisor had told him that his job was on a need to know basis, and as far as the business was concerned, Stanley didn't need to know anything. After a year and a half on the job, the only thing Stanley knew for sure was that his paychecks always cleared at the bank.

To get to work, he had to walk through a storage yard stacked high with lumber, concrete blocks, and steel girders. Concealed in the middle of all the building materials was a stairway leading underground. A single low-wattage light bulb illuminated the dark steps just enough for him to find his way down safely. At the bottom of the stairs he had to pass the same stinking biowaste bin he passed every night. It always had the exact same mixture of foul odors—something chemical, something like rotting food, and most disturbingly, something like how he imagined the smell of decaying flesh. The stench set the tone for the night Stanley was about to spend.

Just like the biowaste bin, Stanley's job stank.

He scanned his ID badge, and the huge metal door opened with a groan that always seemed to express how Stanley felt about his upcoming shift. Sometimes he groaned right along with it.

The facility was dark and lacked proper ventilation. Because of its underground location, there was always a level of dampness in the air that made Stanley feel clammy. Supposedly, the building was a factory, but even on the inside, it provided no clue as to what kind of work might have been going on there. The building was a network of dim hallways faintly illuminated by sickly greenish lights. Networks of black pipes snaked overhead. Throughout the hallways were giant locked metal doors. Stanley had no idea what went on behind them.

If the place were a factory, it would stand to reason that people were on the premises manufacturing something. Sometimes, Stanley could hear the banging and rumbling of some kind of machinery behind the big locked doors. He assumed that there must be other workers in the building, people operating the machinery, but during his entire time on the job, he had yet to lay eyes on another human being.

It was strange to be a guard and not really know what it was you were guarding.

Stanley walked down one of the hallways, hearing hissing and clanging from behind one of the metal doors, and then scanned his ID badge to enter the security office. He settled down at his desk, where he could watch all of the building's entrances and exits on the facility's high-tech monitors.

Stanley had been hired to work at this facility a year and a half ago. At his job interview, it became obvious that this job was unlike any other security guard position he had ever held before. The supervisor who hired him was a strange little bald man in a too-large suit who fidgeted and seemed to have a hard time meeting Stanley's eyes. "It's not a difficult job," the man had said. "You sit in the security office, watch the building's exits on the monitors, and make sure nothing gets out."

"Nothing gets out?" Stanley had asked. "In other jobs, I've always watched to make sure nobody gets *in*."

"Well, this isn't other jobs," the twitchy little man had said, taking a sudden interest in the papers on his desk. "Just watch the exits, and you'll be fine."

"Yes, sir," Stanley had said. He was confused, but he didn't want to make trouble. He had been laid off from his previous position, and the bills were piling up. He needed this job.

"When do you think you can start?" the man had asked him, looking in the general direction of Stanley's face but still not meeting his eyes.

"As soon as you need me, sir." Stanley had been expecting a more rigorous interview. Usually, for security jobs, there were lots of questions, personality tests, references to be followed up on, and an extensive background check. Companies wanted to make sure they weren't hiring the fox to guard the henhouse, as Stanley's granny used to say.

"Excellent," the man had said with what was almost a smile. "We've had a sudden vacancy, I'm afraid, and we are in urgent need of someone to fill the position."

"Guy up and quit on you?" Stanley had asked.

"In a matter of speaking," the man had said, looking past Stanley. "Unfortunately, the prior security guard . . . passed away suddenly. Very tragic."

"What happened to him?" Stanley had asked. He knew

there were inherent dangers in the job, but if the prior guard had been killed in the line of duty, he felt like he ought to be told about it. If this job was especially dangerous, he needed to know what he was signing up for and make an informed decision.

"Massive heart attack, I'm afraid," the man had said, looking down and shuffling some papers on his desk. "We never know how much time we're given, do we?"

"No, sir," Stanley had said, thinking of his dad, whom he had lost recently.

The man had nodded thoughtfully, then looked at Stanley. "But I think you'll find it an easy job. Just keep an eye on those exits, make sure everything that's supposed to be in the building stays in the building, and you'll be fine."

"Yes, sir," Stanley had said. "Thank you." He had reached out to shake the man's cold, bony little hand, and just like that, he had the job.

As a result, Stanley had spent the last year and a half monitoring exits to make sure "nothing got out," even though he wasn't entirely sure what that phrase even meant. Why had the man who'd hired him said "nothing" instead of "nobody"? What exactly was it that Stanley was watching for? He had thought he might ask the strange, twitchy little man about it one day, but since that brief job interview, Stanley had never seen him again.

Stanley unscrewed the lid on his thermos of coffee and got ready for another long, lonely night.

He wouldn't mind the lonely nights so much if his days

weren't lonely, too. Up until two weeks ago, when Amber, his girlfriend for more than two years, dumped him, his days had been brighter. During his dull working hours, Stanley would actually look forward to the time that awaited him once he clocked out at 7:00 a.m. He would walk over to the City Diner across the street for a big breakfast—eggs, bacon, toast, and crusty, oniony hash browns. Once his belly was full, he'd walk back to his apartment and fall into an exhausted sleep for a few hours. Afterward, he would wake up, eat a sandwich, do a little cleaning or laundry, and then play video games until Amber got off work at the grocery store at five.

Amber always brought over ingredients for dinner. She loved the cooking shows on TV and liked to try out new recipes, which was just fine with Stanley. He loved to eat and had the belly to prove it. He wasn't fat, exactly, just well padded, like a comfortable sofa. Spare ribs with plum sauce, chicken adobo, spaghetti carbonara—whatever new recipe Amber wanted to experiment with, Stanley was happy to eat it. Amber and Stanley would cook dinner together, and then they would sit across from each other at his little kitchen table and eat and talk about their days. Since Amber actually saw people at her job, she often had funny stories about things that had happened at the store. After they loaded the dishwasher, they'd cuddle on the couch and watch TV shows or a movie until it was time for Stanley to get ready for work. Most of their dates were cozy nights in, but on Stanley's nights off, they'd go out to dinner—usually to Luigi's Spaghetti House or Wong's Palace—and see a movie or go bowling.

Stanley's time with Amber always felt happy and comfortable, and he had thought she felt the same way. But on the terrible day when she broke up with him, she said, "This relationship is as stagnant as a frog pond. It's not going anywhere."

Blindsided, Stanley had said, "Well, where would you like it to go?"

She had looked at him like his question was part of the problem. "That's just it, Stanley. You shouldn't have to ask."

Stanley was barely twenty-five, and Amber was the first serious girlfriend he had ever had. He loved her and had told her so, but he didn't feel emotionally or financially ready for engagement or marriage. He had thought that what he and Amber had was enough for now. It was too bad she didn't feel that way, too.

A few days before, Stanley had gone to his nephew Max's fifth birthday party at his sister Melissa's house. It was the first time he'd left the house to go anywhere but work since the breakup. At first, the sight of the playful preschoolers and the familiar festiveness of the balloons, cake, and presents had cheered him up a little. He had come in his uniform because he knew Max thought it was cool, and as it turned out the other boys Max's age thought it was cool, too. They had swarmed him saying things like "Your badge is so shiny!" and "Do you chase bad guys?" They were a hoot. Stanley liked little kids. Always had.

After the kids had gone back to their party games, Stanley had listened to the parents who were standing around, talking and laughing about the things their kids said or did. He had started thinking, what if Amber had been his last chance to settle down and have kids and he had blown it? What if he was doomed to always be the bachelor uncle at his nephew's birthday party, standing on the sidelines, and never somebody's husband, somebody's dad?

It didn't help that Todd, Stanley's brother-in-law, had sidled up to him and said, "Hey, man, I was picking up a takeout order at Luigi's the other night and saw your ex on a date with the manager of the Snack Space."

Stanley had nearly choked on his birthday cake. "She's dating somebody else already?"

"It sure looked like a date to me. She probably had him lined up before she even broke up with you," Todd had said. "Do you know the guy?"

Stanley had shaken his head.

"Well, I hate to break it to you, but he's tall and fit. A sharp dresser, too. I checked out his car in the parking lot when I left. A sports car."

Stanley was short and dumpy and didn't own a car, and if he did, it sure wouldn't be anything as expensive as a sports car. Maybe that's why his relationship with Amber had been stagnant. She wanted to climb the social ladder, and he was content where he was.

Stagnant Stanley, he should be called.

He had to stop brooding, he told himself. He was at work, so he should be working. He drank his coffee and monitored the lack of activity in the building. All the exits were clear. They were always clear. He didn't wish for danger, but it would be nice to have something to do.

Even with the caffeine, his eyelids started getting heavy, and his head felt like a bowling ball he was trying to carry on his shoulders. He started to nod off. This was typical. On any given shift, Stanley was likely to spend four of the eight hours fast asleep. That was one reason he didn't try too hard to look for another job despite his boredom and loneliness. How many places would pay you for sleeping? Soon Stanley was snoozing away in his chair, his head lolled back and his big feet propped up on the desk.

Beep! Beep! Beep! Beep!

Stanley was awakened by an alarm. Disoriented for a second, he mistook it for his alarm clock at home, but then he remembered where he was and checked the monitors. A motion sensor had been activated in a vent right there in the security office. Well, at least he wouldn't have to go far to check things out. Stanley stretched, rose from his chair, and grabbed his flashlight.

He squatted on the floor, removed the cover from the vent, and shone the flashlight into the darkness. He saw nothing.

Really, the vent was too small for anything too dangerous to pass through it. Maybe a mouse or a rat had activated the sensor. If the problem continued, he might fill out a report (though he was never really sure who received and read the reports he sent) and suggest that the management call a pest control company.

Stanley yawned and went back to his chair. It was time to get back to his nap.

Two hours later, he woke up with a start. He sat up, wiped the drool from his mouth, and looked at the monitors. Nothing. But on his desk there was an object that hadn't been there before. It wasn't immediately apparent what it was.

Upon closer inspection, it appeared to be a toy—a doll of some kind with jointed arms and legs. It wore a tiny white tutu, and its little feet were painted white so it looked like it was wearing ballet slippers. Its arms were raised like a ballerina who was about to do a pirouette. Stanley smiled to himself at his rudimentary knowledge of ballet terminology. All those times of being dragged to his older sister's ballet recitals as a kid had at least taught him something. The simple jointed doll also reminded him a little of the jointed dolls that had been in his high school art room. The wooden dolls could be arranged in a variety of positions to teach students how to draw the human form. But unlike the art room dolls, which were faceless, this ballerina doll had a face.

But it wasn't the face you would expect.

It would seem logical for a ballerina doll's face to be painted to look like a beautiful girl's. Not this one. Its face was clown white. Its big black eye sockets were blank and empty. It had no discernable nose, but its big black mouth was a toothless, grinning, gaping hole. The face didn't match the body at all. Why would somebody paint a ballerina doll's face in such a ghoulish style?

Stanley's mind was full of questions. What was this weird thing, and what was it doing on his desk? Who had put it there?

He picked up the doll. He spent a few moments bending it into different positions. *Look! Now she's doing the splits! Now she's doing a Russian folk dance!* Stanley chuckled at how easily amused he was. He really did spend way too much time by himself these days. He should get a hobby. He tilted the doll over to make her do a headstand.

A small voice from inside the doll's body said, "We like you!"

"What was that?" Stanley said, tilting the doll over again. It must have some kind of sound chip inside that reacted to movement.

"We like you!" It was a little girl's voice, high-pitched and giggly. Cute.

"Who's *we*?" Stanley said, smiling down at the doll. "I just count one of you." He tilted her.

"I like being close to you!" the doll chirped.

"Well, believe me, it's been a while since a girl said that to me," Stanley said, holding up the doll to look at her better. "Too bad you're tiny and not an actual human being. Kind of weird-looking, too." He tilted her again. He wondered how many recorded phrases were in her vocabulary.

"You're so warm and squishy!" the doll said with a giggle.

Well, that was a new one. But it was true, or at least the squishy part was. He had been eating like an elephant ever since Amber broke up with him. He had always been a big eater, but this was different. Now he was eating because of sadness—whole tubs of chocolate chip cookie dough ice cream, family-size bags of potato chips with French onion dip, half a dozen fast-food tacos in one sitting. Emotional eating, the experts on the Internet called it. Emotional eating had made him a warm, squishy mess. He should start eating healthier—salads and fruit and grilled chicken. And he needed to go back to the gym. He had a gym membership. He just couldn't remember the last time he'd used it . . . maybe before he and Amber got together. "I think you're a good influence on me," he said to the doll, smiling as he tilted it.

"Take me home with you!" the doll said with that same little giggle in her voice.

He set her back on his desk. "I might do that, little dolly," he said. "It's almost like you were left here as a present for me." But who would have left it for him? He looked again at the doll's ballerina body and strange, masklike face. "A weird present, but I don't know . . . I kind of like you." Tilt.

"We like you!" the doll said.

"So the feeling is mutual," Stanley said, chuckling again. He set the doll down and checked the monitors. Nothing at the exits. It was time to finish that nap.

Stanley was at Luigi's Spaghetti House eating at a table by himself. He was cutting the spaghetti into little sticks with his butter knife, which used to drive Amber crazy. You were supposed to twirl it onto your fork, she said, using your spoon to keep the noodles from falling off. To Stanley, this always seemed like an unnecessary delay of getting food into his mouth. He felt the same way about the chopsticks when they ate at Wong's Palace, which Amber always insisted on using while Stanley efficiently shoveled in his General Tso's chicken with a fork.

But Stanley and Amber weren't eating anywhere together anymore. She was sitting at a cozy table in the corner with a handsome, well-dressed man. They were talking and laughing and feeding each other bites off their plates. Stanley felt embarrassed to be sitting at his table alone, but Amber and her date didn't seem to see him. It was like he was invisible. Stanley looked around the dining room to avoid looking at Amber and her new boyfriend. At the head of the room, where there was usually a piano, was a casket. Stanley's dad lay inside it, his sunken cheeks too rosy with makeup where the mortician had tried to disguise his death pallor.

Everywhere he looked, Stanley saw someone he had loved and lost. He looked down at his plate to avoid seeing anyone else. His spaghetti had turned into a tangle of writhing, wriggling worms. "The worms crawl in, the worms crawl out/They eat your guts and *they spit them out . . ."* Stanley remembered the gruesome song from the playground when he was a kid. It was morbid, sure, but what did they know of death back then? But now his childhood was gone, his dad was gone, Amber was gone . . . why did everything good have to go away? He picked up the plate of worms and hurled it across the room. The plate shattered against the wall and left a red smear of spaghetti sauce studded with chopped-up noodles.

Stanley woke up gasping for breath. *It's okay,* he told himself. *It was just a bad dream.* It was five minutes until his shift was over, and the doll that had been on his desk was gone. It was strange. Nobody but him was ever in here. Who would have come into the security office and taken it? Maybe the same person who had come in and left it in the first place—whoever that was.

For a split second he considered filing a report about it but realized there was no way he could. What would it say? *Fell asleep at my post at 3:02 a.m. Woke to find a doll on my desk. Fell back asleep, woke up, and it was gone.* That was a quick way to get fired.

If Amber were still around, he would have a story to tell about something interesting that happened at work for once. These were some of the saddest moments of Stanley's already sad days, when he'd think, *Wait till I tell Amber!* and then remember that there was no Amber to tell.

Stanley held his nose as he passed the biowaste bin outside the facility. He emerged from the stairs to a day that was bright and sunny. After staying in a dark hole for eight hours, it always took his eyes a few minutes to adjust to the intensity of daylight. He squinted and blinked, like a mole that had just popped up from its underground tunnel.

Stanley crossed the street to the City Diner, sat down in his usual red-vinyl booth, and turned his upside-down coffee cup into the upright position. Almost as if by magic, Katie the server was there to fill it. Stanley knew a little bit about Katie from making small talk with her. She was around his age and was taking some classes at the community college now that her son had started preschool. "You want the usual this morning, Stan?" she asked. Her smile was friendly, and her eyes were very blue. She was prettier than Stanley remembered her being.

Maybe he was just lonely. Since the breakup, he would often go for whole days in which Katie was the only other human being he talked to.

"Actually, I think I might take a look at a menu today, Katie." If he was going to make healthier choices, he might as well start now, though it was hard to do with the irresistible smell of bacon wafting through the diner. Watching what other people were eating didn't help, either. The guy at the booth across from him was eating a tall, golden, butter-and-maple-syrup-drenched stack of pancakes. They looked delicious.

Katie handed him the laminated folder. "Changing it up this morning, are we?"

"I thought I might." He scanned the menu, looking for healthier options. None of them sounded as tasty as his usual order, but if he was going to get less "squishy," he was going to have to make some sacrifices. "I think I'll take the mushroom egg-white omelet with the turkey sausage and whole-wheat toast."

Katie smiled as she wrote down his order. "I'm impressed. Going on a diet, are we?"

He smiled and patted his belly. "I'm thinking about it."

After Katie left to put in his order, Stanley let his gaze wander around the restaurant. In the last booth in the corner, an old man sat nursing a cup of coffee and reading the newspaper. He was at the City Diner every morning, always alone, lingering over coffee long after his breakfast plate had been cleared. Stanley could feel the old man's loneliness just as surely as he could feel his own. He wondered, now that Amber had dumped him, if his fate was the same as the old man's. Would he grow old and be so lonely that he sat for hours in public places just to have the illusion of some company?

Wasn't that what Stanley himself was doing right now?

"Here you go," Katie said, delivering his breakfast with a smile.

The egg-white omelet was surprisingly decent, but when Stanley tried to eat his whole-wheat toast, he had difficulty swallowing it. His throat had gotten sore suddenly and felt as if it must be swollen partially shut. It was odd. He couldn't remember the last time he'd had a sore throat. He pushed his breakfast plate away.

"Does the healthy stuff not taste as good?" Katie asked,

clearing his dishes. "You're usually a member of the clean-plate club."

"No, it was good," Stanley said, his voice coming out croaky. "My throat's just really sore. Makes it hard to eat."

"Well, there are all kinds of bugs going around. Lots of kids and teachers are out sick at my little boy's preschool. I hope you're not coming down with something," Katie said.

"Me too," Stanley said. But it was entirely possible that he was. Who knew how many germs were swirling around that damp, dark underground facility that no fresh air or sunlight ever reached?

On the way home, he stopped at the drugstore and bought some sore throat lozenges. He popped one as soon as he had paid for them. Swallowing was becoming more and more painful and difficult.

When Amber had come over on a daily basis, Stanley had kept his apartment reasonably clean. Now when he walked into it, it felt like a doubly nasty surprise. There was the mess, but there was also the meaning behind the mess: it was a reminder that Amber was gone. The coffee table was cluttered with half-empty soda cans, hamburger wrappers, fried chicken boxes, and Chinese takeout containers. Dirty laundry was scattered in random piles on the floor. Part of him wanted to clean it up, but the rest of him said, *What does it even matter? She's not coming back, and there's nobody here but me to see the mess.*

Stanley unwrapped a throat lozenge and popped it in his mouth. He was definitely getting sick. Great. That was just what he needed. One more thing to make his life a little more miserable.

His mom had always been a big believer in steam when he or his sister was coming down with a cold, so he decided to take a hot shower. If congestion was what was causing his sore throat, breathing in some steam might help. Taking off his security uniform shirt, he had a hard time pulling his left arm out of the sleeve. Once he finally got his shirt off, he could see the problem. His left arm was swollen to nearly twice the size of his right one. The arm felt weird, too. Numb, like when a foot "falls asleep." He shook his arm around, trying to wake it up, but it still lacked sensation.

What kind of bizarre illness gave you a sore throat and a numb, swollen arm? He was no doctor, but he knew those two symptoms didn't go together.

Stanley turned up the shower temperature as hot as he could stand it. When he held his left arm under the nozzle's spray, he could feel neither the heat nor the jets of water hitting his skin. After he got out of the shower, he put on a T-shirt and sweatpants, took two ibuprofen, popped another lozenge, and crawled into bed. Whatever this illness was, maybe rest would fix it.

He slept for eight hours, a dark, dreamless sleep. When he woke up, his throat felt like someone had cut it. He clutched his neck and drew his hand away and looked at it, almost expecting to see blood. He sat up slowly, his head fuzzy, achy, and disoriented. His left arm was still numb and felt heavy and weak, a leaden object that he was forced to drag around but was of no use to him.

He popped another throat lozenge even though the first one hadn't begun to touch his level of pain. In the bathroom, he looked at himself in the mirror. His eyes were bloodshot, and he looked like he hadn't slept for days even though he should have been well rested. A sore throat . . . what did his mom used to give him for a sore throat when he was a kid? He flashed back to days when he would stay home sick from school and his mom would take care of him. Hot tea with lemon and honey—that was what she had always made for him. He was pretty sure he had some tea bags somewhere. He went to the kitchen and rummaged through the cabinets until he found a box of tea bags that had been there since who knows when. *Tea doesn't expire, does it?* he thought.

He microwaved a cup of water and submerged the tea bag in it. He found a little plastic packet of honey in the drawer that was full of restaurant takeout packets of mustard, ketchup, and soy sauce. He stirred the honey into the tea. He remembered his mom saying the honey was soothing because it coated your throat. He didn't remember what the lemon was for, but he would have to do without it.

He turned on the TV to check sports scores and sipped his hot drink. It helped a little bit. When he finished, he went back to the kitchen and opened a can of chicken noodle soup. Chicken soup was supposed to be good for sick people, right? He heated the soup on the stove, then took a bowl of it into the living room to eat in front of the TV. He quickly discovered that all he could manage was sipping the broth. The chicken chunks and noodles hurt too much going down. It felt like he was swallowing rocks.

Stanley took more ibuprofen and sucked on another throat lozenge and hoped that he would feel better as the evening wore on. But the feeling of pain in his throat didn't go away any more than the feeling of anything in his left arm came back. He toyed with the idea of calling in sick, but he knew he couldn't miss out on eight hours of pay. Money was too tight. He barely had enough for rent and groceries as it was. When he put on his uniform, the left sleeve of his shirt was so tight he could barely bend his elbow.

It was not an easy walk to work, with his painful throat and his lifeless left arm, but eventually he made it to the storage yard and down the hidden stairs. As usual, he held his breath passing the stinking biowaste bin and scanned his ID badge at the door. In the facility, he let his eyes adjust to the dim greenish light for a moment before heading to the security office. He checked the monitors and saw nothing out of the ordinary. Good. He was tired and in pain and ready for a nap. He leaned back in his chair and let the welcome oblivion of sleep overtake him.

He awoke with a gasp, feeling like he was being watched. He looked around and checked the monitors. Nothing.

But the doll was on his desk again.

He picked it up and smiled at it. "You again?" he said. His voice was getting hoarser. "Where did you come from? Is somebody playing a game with me?" Maybe he had a secret admirer, he thought, but he immediately dismissed the idea as ridiculous. What kind of weirdo secret admirer would leave him a ballerina doll? Not the kind of secret admirer he'd want, that's for sure. He tilted the doll over to activate her voice.

"We like you," she chirped in her happy little-girl tone.

"I like you, too, little dolly," Stanley said. "I'm not sure why I do, but I do." Maybe having the talking doll there with him at work was like people who kept the TV on in the background all the time in their homes. A little bit of noise was a reminder that even if it didn't feel that way, you weren't all alone in the world. Sad but understandable. The world was a lonely place. He turned over the doll again.

"Take me home with you," she said.

"Well, I was going to take you home with me yesterday, but when I woke up, you were gone. I guess you missed your chance, huh? Who do you belong to anyway?" He tilted her.

"Take me home with you."

He examined the doll. "Maybe you belong to the kid of somebody else who works here. I don't want to take away some kid's toy. You'd be better off with a little girl than with me." Tilt.

"Take me home with you," the doll said again.

Too bad real women weren't this insistent on having his company. "Some little girl could be real upset if her dolly's gone. And I'm a big grown man. I don't have any use for dollies." So why was he talking to this doll as if it could understand what he said and making his throat sorer in the process? This virus or whatever it was must be making him loopy, he thought. And here he went again, tilting the thing to hear what it would say.

"Take me home with you."

He set the doll down on the desk. It had officially crossed the line from cute to annoying. "Okay, okay. If you stay put on this desk until my shift is over, I'll take you home with me. But now it's nap time. Nighty night." He leaned back in his chair and dozed off again.

Stanley was running late for work. He was trying to get ready, but his big fat fingers were too clumsy to button the shirt of his uniform or tie his shoes. He needed help, but he was utterly alone. Finally, knowing he would be terribly late if he didn't leave right away, he ran out onto the street in his half-buttoned shirt and untied shoes. But when he looked around, all of the familiar landmarks of his neighborhood were gone. Where was Greenblatt's Deli? Where was the Dutch Girl Dry Cleaner's? He looked up at a street sign and saw that the street names had changed. The sign that had once said "Forrest Avenue" now said "Fazbear Avenue." It made no sense, but he was lost. How could that be when he was just ten steps from the door of his apartment building?

Finally, he hailed a cab and told the driver the address of the storage yard that hid his place of employment. None of the streets or buildings looked familiar as he rode through the city, but the driver seemed to know where he was going. Stanley told himself to breathe and relax. It was okay; things were under control now.

The cab stopped on a dark side street that Stanley didn't recognize. Maybe the cab driver didn't know where he was going after all. "Hey, buddy," Stanley said. "I don't think you've got the right address."

When the cab driver turned around, his face wasn't human. It was a bizarre robotic version of an animal's face, pink and white with a long snout, large ears, and glowing yellow eyes. The face, apparently hinged, split open, revealing the full orbs of the creature's eyes and a mouthful of knifelike teeth. It opened its jaws wider and lunged toward Stanley in the back seat, shattering the panel of glass that separated them.

Had he screamed? Stanley wondered as he tried to shake off the nightmare. Probably his sore throat had rendered him so hoarse that he couldn't have screamed if he had tried. But even if he had, who would have heard him, squirreled away in his tiny, dark office? He could die in here, and nobody would notice. Nobody guards the security guard.

What was that thing in his dream, anyway?

When he finally woke all the way and could reorient himself to his familiar surroundings, he noticed that the doll was gone again. It was weird. He kind of wanted to tell someone about it, but who would he tell?

At the City Diner, Katie filled his coffee cup. "You look like you could use this," she said.

Stanley winced as he tried to swallow a sip of the scalding liquid. Coffee was probably a bad idea.

"You want your usual, or do you want to go the healthy route again?" she asked.

"Oatmeal," Stanley said, his voice a scratchy croak. "Just a bowl of oatmeal."

Katie knitted her brow. "Are you okay, Stan? You don't sound so good." It was nice that she cared enough to ask.

"Sore throat's worse." He rubbed his neck. "Don't think I can eat solid food."

"Okay. Oatmeal it is. But have you seen a doctor? You know, the drugstore around the corner has a little walk-in clinic. When I had an ear infection last month, they gave me some medicine that fixed me right up. They're pretty inexpensive, too."

"No. No doctors." People always thought doctors could fix everything. But when Stanley's dad had gotten so sick he couldn't work anymore, he had gone to the doctor and taken every medicine and done every torturous treatment he had been told to do. Within six months, he was dead anyway.

"It's actually a nurse instead of a doctor at the clinic," Katie said. "She's really nice. She'll just ask you some questions, take a look at your ears, nose, and throat, and then write you a prescription."

"It's just some kind of bug. It'll run its course," Stanley rasped. He had to admit he did sound terrible, though.

"Suit yourself," Katie said. "I'll get you your oatmeal. And I'm also bringing you a large orange juice on the house. A little extra vitamin C can't hurt."

"Thank you." Stanley was struck by how caring Katie was. He wondered if she was single. It would be nice to have someone who cared about him.

Eating the oatmeal felt like swallowing hot sand. Hoping for relief, he sipped some orange juice, but it burned his throat like battery acid. On his way home, he stopped at the drugstore and bought some throat lozenges that were supposed to be stronger than the ones he had been using. He doubted they would be strong enough. Once he was back in his apartment, he kicked off his shoes and collapsed on the bed without even taking off his uniform. He was asleep in seconds.

He awoke seven hours later to a ringing phone. His mouth was dry as dust, and his throat stung and burned. He reached for the phone with his good arm but quickly discovered that it was numb and swollen now, too. Awkwardly, he managed to lift the phone and put it to his ear. "Hello?" His voice was a scratchy whisper.

"Stan? Is that you?" It was his older sister, Melissa.

"Yeah. Hi, sis." He hadn't seen her since his nephew's birthday party, but usually she called from time to time to check on him.

"You sound awful." Stanley could hear the worry in her voice. "Are you sick?"

"Come down with a cold," he said. He didn't want to

say any more than the minimum number of words it took to communicate meaning. Talking hurt too much.

"No wonder," Melissa said. "Working nights in that dark, airless factory. Like being in the catacombs. I'm surprised you're not sick all the time. Hey, listen, the kids are over at Mom's, and Todd is bowling tonight. I made a pot of chili and some corn bread. I thought I might bring some over, and we could have dinner together."

Even though he felt horrible, he was still grateful for the offer of company. At least he didn't have to face another evening alone. "Sounds nice," he rasped.

"Okay, I'll be by at six. Do you need me to pick you up anything from the drugstore?"

A new throat, Stanley thought, but he said, "No thanks."

With difficulty, he dragged himself out of bed and into the bathroom. He looked in the mirror to survey the damage, which was quite significant. Dark shadows had formed under his bloodshot eyes, and his skin had an unhealthy grayish cast. What worried him most, though, was his right arm. Like his left, it was now so swollen that the sleeve of his uniform was like the casing of a fat sausage. He didn't know if he'd be able to take the shirt off without ripping it. Probably best just to leave it on for now.

He splashed some water on his face and managed to control his numb right arm enough to run a comb through his hair and squeeze some toothpaste onto his toothbrush. Brushing his teeth was so excruciating that tears sprang to his eyes. His throat felt like an open wound, and the inside of his mouth was also raw and inflamed. When he rinsed his mouth and spat out the water, it was streaked with red ribbons of blood. He looked at himself in the mirror again. The grooming he had been able to manage hadn't made much of an improvement. His chin and jaw were shadowed with stubble, but he didn't trust his numb arm enough to use a razor. This would have to do. He staggered to the living room and flopped on the couch, unable to find even enough energy to pick up the TV remote.

Melissa, who had been a responsible person seemingly since birth, arrived at six on the dot as promised, carrying a large metal pot and one of the recycled tote bags she used for groceries. Her curly brown hair was pulled back in a neat ponytail, and she was still wearing the button-down shirt and khakis she wore to work. "Hey, bro," she said, walking in the door. Her greeting was followed by, "Yikes! What happened here?"

Stanley knew things were messy, but he hadn't really given the appearance of the apartment much thought. Seeing it through Melissa's eyes, though, he knew it was a disaster area. He was embarrassed but didn't want to show it. He sat back on the couch and tried for a nonchalant shrug. "Amber broke up with me," he croaked.

"Yeah, I know that," she said, looking around with the same repulsed expression she'd had when she was a little girl and he had put worms in her hair. "But what happened to this place? Amber wasn't the one who cleaned it, was she?"

"No, I did. I just started caring less once she stopped coming over." Without Amber, cleaning didn't seem worth the effort. Few things did.

Melissa's look shifted from disgust to sympathy. "Poor little bro. Hang on, let me put this chili on the stove to heat up." She disappeared into the apartment's tiny kitchen, then reemerged holding a handful of trash bags. "It's kinda bad in there, too. Are all your dishes dirty?"

"Pretty much," Stanley said.

Melissa took a deep breath. "Okay, here's what I'm going to do for you. I'm going to gather up all these cans and bottles and load them in my car to take to the recycling center. I'm going to hold my nose and gather up the trash and throw it away. And then I'm going to load your dishwasher and run it and hand-wash any other dirty dishes that are left over." She looked down at the random pieces of clothing that had been tossed on the floor. "I draw the line at touching your dirty socks and underwear. Those are your problem."

"Fair enough," Stanley croaked. "Thank you. I wish I could help." His arms were so weak and heavy he couldn't imagine picking up anything.

"No, you rest. You look like Death holding a cracker, as Granny used to say." She dropped an old fried chicken box into the trash bag.

Stanley let himself smile a little. "Yeah, I never understood that expression. Why would Death be holding a cracker?"

"I never got it, either," Melissa said. "Why would the Grim Reaper need to snack? Isn't he just basically a skeleton?" She looked around the room like a general figuring out a plan of attack. "Listen, I'm going to make you a cup of tea with honey and lemon like Mom used to make us, and then I'll really get going on this cleaning."

"I don't have any lemons," Stanley rasped.

"I brought the tea, the lemon, and the honey," Melissa said.

Of course she did. "You think of everything," Stanley said.

Melissa smiled. "I try my best."

When they were little, Melissa had always organized what games they would play and how they would play them. At the time, he had thought that tendency was bossy and annoying, but now he saw it had its good points, especially now that his life had descended into chaos.

In a few minutes, Stanley was sitting with a mug of tea in his hands while Melissa launched a one-woman offensive against all the garbage in the living room. "You're amazing," he said. If he couldn't help her, at least he could praise her.

"Well, it's nice to have an appreciative audience. My kids sure aren't," Melissa said, wrinkling her nose as she picked up an old Chinese food container between her forefinger and thumb and dropped it into a trash bag. "Yeesh, I wonder what that used to be."

"Lo mein, I think," Stanley said. He winced as he took a swallow of tea. "I'm sorry I let things get so bad. It's not your job to clean up after me."

"No, it's not," Melissa said, tossing some wadded-up taco wrappers into the trash bag. "But it is my job to make sure you're okay, and I haven't been doing my job."

"That's not true. You've called me—"

"Yes, I've called you several times since the breakup to make sure you're okay, and you've always said yes. And you showed up at Max's birthday party, which I thought was a good sign. But clearly I should've come over earlier and checked things out here." She knotted the top of the already-full garbage bag. "Because you, little brother of mine, are definitely not okay."

"No, I'm not," he half whispered. He felt like he might cry, which would be embarrassing, crying in front of his big sister like he was a baby again. Stanley wasn't usually a crier. He hadn't cried since their dad had died. But looking at his messy life through Melissa's eyes, he could see how bad it was. Her life was so well balanced—she had a college degree, a job she liked at the courthouse, a nice husband, and two kids she was utterly devoted to. Compared to her life, his was pathetic and empty. And his throat hurt so, so much that the pain alone almost brought tears to his eyes.

Melissa must've sensed his distress because she patted him on the shoulder and said, "I'll tell you what. Let me take a break from cleaning and get us some dinner. The chili should be hot by now, and you might feel a little better once you've had something to eat."

Stanley sniffled and nodded.

The chili was a family recipe, and it was usually one of Stanley's favorite meals. He was generally good for at least two bowls full—sometimes even three. But tonight, even though the chili was perfect and had shredded cheddar cheese on top and corn bread on the side the way he liked it, he couldn't eat much. The peppery broth burned going down, making it feel like someone was holding a lit match to his already inflamed throat.

"This is not the Stan I know," Melissa said when he pushed aside his mostly full bowl. "Do you remember what Mom used to call you at meal times?"

Stan smiled a little. "Her big hungry boy."

"She used to say you must have a hollow leg because she couldn't see where you put it all." Melissa cleared their bowls and started loading the dishwasher with two weeks' worth of dirty cups, plates, and silverware. "Listen, I know you're going to argue with me about this, but why don't you let me make an appointment for you with the doctor Todd and the kids and I see? She's really nice and easy to talk to."

"No doctors," Stanley croaked. An unwanted image popped into his mind of his dad in his hospital bed, pale and skeletally thin, tethered to plastic tubes that snaked all over his body.

Melissa rolled her eyes. "Yeah, I knew you'd say that.

Look, I know you've never liked going to the doctor, and you stopped going once you got too old for Mom to make you. Then you got even weirder about doctors after Dad got sick—"

"It's not weird," Stanley said. "The doctors made him sicker, then he died. Chemotherapy, radiation—they pumped him full of poison."

Melissa shook her head. This was an old argument between them. "Stan, Dad knew something was wrong and he waited too long to get medical attention. Months and months. By the time he saw a doctor, it was too late to help him. They gave the chemo a try, but the cancer had already spread. It probably would've worked if they'd gotten to it earlier." She looked him in the eye. "And now you're being too stubborn to go to the doctor, too. It's like it's some kind of weird family tradition. Well, it's not one we should keep up."

"I don't have cancer," Stanley rasped. At least he had that going for him. "I'll be okay."

"I know you don't have cancer," Melissa said, "but you have a weird combination of symptoms. Your throat's sore, and your arms look all stiff and swollen. Maybe it's just some kind of random virus, but I think you ought to get it checked out."

"It'll clear up," Stanley said. He knew it was a weird combination of symptoms, too, but he wasn't going to admit it to her.

Melissa sighed. "I tell you what. I'm going to come over

and check on you in three days, and if you're not better by then, I'm taking you to the doctor even if I have to get Todd and his big burly friends from the bowling league to help me drag you there."

"Okay," Stanley said because he knew from experience that ultimately there was no arguing with his big sister. "Three days."

Within an hour, Melissa had picked up all the empty bottles and cans and washed all his dirty dishes. Except for the dirty laundry on the floor, the living room was now clutter-free. "Well, that's some improvement anyway," she said, looking around at the newly clean surfaces.

"I can't thank you enough," Stanley rasped. He was amazed at all the work she had gotten done while he sat on the couch doing exactly nothing.

"I don't want you to thank me," Melissa said, putting on her jacket. "What I do want you to do is call in sick to work tonight and get some rest."

"I'll think about it," he said, knowing he couldn't afford to pass up the money.

"Don't think about it. *Do it*." Melissa leaned over the couch and gave him a quick hug. "And remember, if you're not better in three days, I'm taking you to the doctor."

"I remember." He knew she wasn't going to let him forget.

"Okay, I'll get out of your hair now." She patted the top of his head. "What you have left of it."

Stanley laughed. He had definitely inherited their father's receding hairline. "You always were the mean one."

Stanley had no intention of calling in sick to work. Since he already had his uniform on, he didn't need to do much to get ready after Melissa left. True, the walk to work was more tiring than usual. His throat burned and stung, and his numb, swollen arms were so heavy he was practically dragging them like a ball and chain. Still, he made it. And now here he was again, descending the hidden stairs and passing the stinking biowaste bin to arrive at his dark, subterranean workplace.

Stanley made his way down the dim hallway. The greenish light gave his already pale skin an even sicklier cast. He scanned his ID badge and settled at his desk in the security office to check the monitors. As always, there was nothing unusual. It was the least demanding job ever. He knew his sister wanted him to stay at home and rest, but why not come to work where he could nap and get paid for it? He leaned back in his chair and was soon snoring lightly.

When the pain in his throat woke him a couple of hours later, the ballerina doll was on his desk again.

It was weird the way the thing kept showing up like that, only to disappear again. He really ought to ask someone about it, but he never saw anyone to ask.

Out of habit, he picked up the doll and tilted it.

"We like you," it said.

He studied the doll's empty eyes and black gaping grin. Really, who thought it was a good idea, making a doll that looked like this? "Yeah, yeah, yeah, so you keep saying," he said.

Where had the doll come from? Who had manufactured it? Had it been made here in the factory? He turned it over to see if he could find a stamp of some kind on it.

"Take me home with you," the doll said.

"See, you keep saying that, too, but whenever I'm ready to go home, you're always gone. You're sending me mixed messages, little dolly," Stanley said. He really ought to conserve his voice. It was barely above a whisper. He tilted the doll again.

"Take me home with you."

Stanley set the doll down on the desk and reached for another throat lozenge. "I tell you what. I can't take you home if you keep disappearing, but if you stay put and are still on the desk when I wake up, you can come home with me." *That's great, Stanley,* he thought. *Try to reason with an inanimate object.* He was in some sorry shape. He leaned back in his chair and closed his eyes.

Stanley was at work, but for some reason the greenish lights that usually provided the building's only illumination had been turned off. He remembered a school field trip to a cave. The tour guide had explained that the fish in the cave's underground pond had no eyes because even if they did have them, it would be too dark for them to see anything. The building was dark like that.

His flashlight was the only thing that made it possible for him to find his way down the hall. He shined it on the walls, on the metal doors, on the floor ahead of him, creating small circles of light in the darkness. Was the whole building without electricity? he wondered. It must not be because he could still hear the rumbling and clanging of the machinery behind the locked metal doors.

He had a strong feeling that something was not right. He needed to get to the office to see if the security monitors were working or if they were down due to the power outage. If they were, he guessed he would have to walk around in the dark and check that each exit was secure. He shined his flashlight ahead. It lit up the sign reading "Security Office" on his door. The scanner for his security badge wasn't working, so he used the key he kept in case of emergency.

The security office was as dark as the rest of the building. All the monitors were down. He shined the flashlight around the room, letting its beam rest on familiar objects: the desk, the chair, the filing cabinet. He moved the flashlight's beam toward the left corner of the room.

The beam illuminated a face. The face did not belong to a human.

It was the face of a cartoon animal—a bear, maybe?—wearing a bow tie and a top hat. As Stanley shined his light on it, the two sides of the face swung open like double doors to reveal a hideous metallic skull made of snaking wires and cables. It stared at Stanley with blank, bulging eyes and sprang at him, its jaws snapping.

Stanley woke with a start. He had never had nightmares like he'd experienced these last few nights while napping at work. What were these strange mechanical creatures that were haunting his dreams? Were these terrors caused by his sadness at losing Amber, or were they symptoms of his physical illness? Or maybe the two things were connected. One thing was for sure: he had never been so physically and emotionally unwell at the same time.

He looked down at his desk. It was bare. The doll hadn't followed his orders to stay put.

Stanley stood up and stretched. He shook his head as if doing so might unscramble his confused brain.

Of course the doll hadn't followed his orders to stay put, he thought—because it was a doll. It couldn't understand what he was saying. No matter how many times it said otherwise, the doll didn't really want to go home with him—it didn't *want* anything because it wasn't alive, and the words it seemed to say were just set, prerecorded noises. None of this explained, though, how the doll showed up on his desk and then disappeared. It couldn't move on its own, so who was putting it there and taking it away? Was somebody playing some kind of prank?

But who would play a prank on Stanley? To his knowledge, nobody else who worked here had ever even seen him.

After his shift, Stanley skipped the City Diner. He would have kind of liked to see Katie, but his throat hurt too much to eat anything, and the thought of food nauseated him. He caught a glimpse of his reflection in a store window. Gray, sweaty, stubbly face and swollen, limp arms. No doubt about it—if he were holding only a cracker, he would look exactly like Death.

He thought of Katie recommending the nurse at the walk-in clinic. Maybe he should stop there. Nurses weren't the same as doctors; he remembered the school nurse when he was a kid as being very kind. He had to do something. He couldn't go on feeling this bad.

The nurse was indeed nice—a blonde, maternal woman who was around his actual mom's age. As soon as she saw him, she said, "Wow, you feel terrible, don't you?"

"Is it that obvious?" Stanley asked. His voice was weak and husky.

The nurse nodded. "Sore throat?"

"Yes, ma'am. A bad one." He didn't tell her about his numb arm. He was too afraid of what she might say. He didn't want to end up in a hospital. When his dad had gone to the hospital, he didn't get out alive.

"Well, let's have a look at you and see if we can get you feeling better." She gestured for him to follow her into the tiny exam room in the back of the drugstore.

She stuck a thermometer in his ear and read the results. "No fever. But I still think we'd better swab your throat and test for strep."

The test wasn't pleasant. She told him to open his mouth wide and came at him with a long-handled Q-tip, which she plunged into his mouth and down his throat.

The soft cotton was as painful as sharp metal against his irritated throat, and he gagged. When she pulled out the big Q-tip, the cotton was dotted with blood.

"Well, that's not good," she said, knitting her brow. "Let me run this test, and then we'll figure out what to do."

In a few minutes, she came back. "No strep, but as irritated as your throat is, I think there's at least some infection. And the blood is worrying. I'm going to write you a prescription for some antibiotics, but if you're not seeing a difference by Monday, I want you to promise me you'll go see your regular doctor."

"I promise," Stanley said, despite the fact that he didn't have a regular doctor and had no plans to get one.

Even though he still felt physically awful walking home, he was also a little hopeful. He had taken action. He had real medicine now. Surely that would fix things.

Stanley looked at himself in the bathroom mirror. It wasn't pretty. He had been wearing his uniform for almost forty-eight hours. He was pale and sweaty, and he smelled as bad as that biowaste bin he passed every day. The uniform had to go. He unbuttoned the shirt, then unbuttoned the cuffs of his sleeves. He pulled on his left sleeve, but his arm was so swollen that it was tightly packed inside the tube of fabric. The right arm was no better. He pulled his sleeve and twisted his torso, hoping he could find some magical position that would make his arms break free of their polyester prison.

Finally, out of desperation, he grabbed a pair of scissors. He slid one blade under his left sleeve. It was a tight fit, but he got it into an angle such that he could snip the sleeve open up the length of his arm. Though working left-handed was more difficult, he did the same with the other sleeve and shucked off the sweaty ruined shirt. It wasn't even his shirt. The company owned the uniforms and loaned them out to employees. The cost was definitely going to come out of his paycheck.

He was unsteady on his feet in the shower and leaned against the wall to keep from slipping and falling. He let the hot water pound on his back in hopes that it would relieve some tension. He felt nothing—neither the heat nor the water—in his swollen left and right arms.

Exhausted from the Herculean effort that undressing and showering had become, Stanley grabbed a T-shirt and some pajama pants. He painfully forced one of the antibiotic pills down his throat with a tiny sip of water and then collapsed into bed.

When he woke up and tried to stand, he immediately fell to the floor. His right leg wasn't bearing weight like a leg was supposed to. As soon as he attempted standing, it crumpled beneath him as if it had no muscles or bones. Sitting on the floor, Stanley touched his right thigh and felt nothing. He slapped it, then punched it hard with his fist. Still nothing. The arm and hand he had used for punching were numb, too. What was happening to him?

Was it some kind of degenerative disease that might leave him in a wheelchair for the rest of his life? But if it was, wasn't it kind of strange for a degenerative disease to progress this rapidly? Maybe going to the walk-in clinic hadn't been enough. Maybe he should let Melissa make him a doctor's appointment. He probably needed to see some kind of specialist. Even if the doctor hurt him, it couldn't be worse than what he was feeling now. He wondered if, like his dad, he had already waited until it was too late to get help.

With great effort, Stanley turned around, put his hands on the bed, and pulled himself to standing. He walked in a slow shuffle, dragging his right leg behind him and letting his left leg do most of the work.

How long had it been since he had eaten or drunk anything? He couldn't remember. Water. He at least had to have water. He shuffled to the kitchen, still clean from Melissa's efforts, and got a glass from the cabinet. He filled it with water from the tap and tried to drink.

Agony. Swallowing even a sip of cool water felt like swallowing ground-up glass. He retched over the sink, bringing up water pink with blood. He had thought he might try to heat up some soup, but if he couldn't even drink, eating was out of the question. And the very thought of swallowing anything hot was unbearable.

His phone rang, making him remember, miserably, that he had left it in the bedroom. He dragged himself toward the insistent ringing, but by the time he got there, it had stopped. The caller ID said "Mom." He knew what she was like. If he didn't call her back, she would automatically think he was dead.

"Hello? Stanley?" She answered on the first ring.

"Hi, Mom." Stanley tried to make his voice sound normal, but it came out husky with a little mouselike squeak at the end.

"You sound terrible."

"Yeah, people keep saying that." He lay down on the bed to talk. No need to waste the energy it took to sit upright.

"Melissa came over to pick up the kids after she was at your place last night. She said you were a wreck."

"That's nice to hear." There was nothing like knowing your mom and your sister had been talking about what a loser you are.

"It's not something to joke around about, Stanley." His mom was using her stern voice, the one she had mastered when he used to get into trouble as a kid. "She thinks you need to go to a doctor."

"I went to a walk-in clinic this morning, Mom. The nurse wrote me a prescription for some pills. They've just not had time to work yet. I'm going to be fine." He didn't really believe he was going to be anywhere in the neighborhood of "fine," but he didn't want to scare his mom. She had gone through so much fear and worry when his dad was sick, she deserved to live the rest of her life in peace.

"Melissa also says she thinks you should get out more,

see some people. Once you're better, of course. She says you're lonely."

"She's probably right. It's just hard. I'm not over Amber yet." He felt a lump forming in his already painful throat. Just what he needed. To cry to his mommy.

"Of course you're not over her, sweetie! It's only been two weeks. But over time, your heart will heal, and there'll be somebody else. Somebody who appreciates you for who you are. I know I'm biased, but I never thought that Amber was good enough for you. You know, I never thought I'd date again after your father died, but a year and a half later, I met Harold. And you have to admit Harold's a really nice guy."

"He is, Mom." Stanley hadn't wanted to like Harold at first; he had felt like it would be disloyal to his dad's memory. But Harold was good to his mom and kept her from getting too lonesome. They went out to dinner every Friday night. On Sundays they walked in the park if it was sunny or in the mall if it was rainy. They always held hands on their walks, which Stanley thought was sweet. He was glad they had each other.

"Now, do you need me to come over there and bring you some soup or some groceries or something?" his mom asked.

"No thanks, Mom. I just need to take my medicine and rest." He didn't want her to see how bad he looked. He knew if she did, she would be dragging him to the emergency room.

"Okay, but I'm going to call you tomorrow to check on you. And if you need me to come over, I will."

"Thanks, Mom."

"And if you're not better by the day after tomorrow, do you promise you'll let Melissa make you an appointment with her doctor?"

He knew it was no use to argue with her. Melissa had inherited her stubbornness from their mom. "I promise."

"I love you, Stanley."

"I love you, too, Mom." Saying these words made him feel sad and vulnerable. If he was going to be this sick, he almost wished he could be a little boy again. He could stay in bed in his jammies, and his mom could take care of him and bring him hot tea and chocolate pudding and comic books. Nobody ever took care of you like that once you were an adult.

After he hung up, he knew he couldn't stay on the bed. If he did, he would pass back out and not make it into work. With one hand on the wall for support, he limped into the living room, fell onto the couch, and turned on the TV. Supposedly he was checking sports scores, but he couldn't focus enough to follow them. He just stared blankly at the lights and colors on the screen, thinking only of how much his throat hurt and how fast his body was failing him. It was like he had turned into a decrepit old man overnight.

All too soon, it was time to get ready for work. When he pulled on his uniform pants, the right leg was too tight.

It looked weird, having one normal pant leg and one that squeezed his thigh like a pair of ladies' tights. His uniform shirt was still in a ripped-up pile on his bedroom floor. He decided he would just wear his plain white T-shirt to work and then try to find a replacement uniform shirt in the storage room when he got there. Or not. What did it matter? No one saw him there anyway. He could go to work in his underwear and nobody would be the wiser.

Since the prospect of walking to work seemed impossible, he decided to take the bus instead. The short walk to the bus stop was difficult enough, and once the bus arrived, he could barely lift his numb and swollen leg high enough to step into the vehicle. He could feel the people behind him shifting from foot to foot and waiting impatiently. As he stumbled to his seat, the other passengers looked at him with concern. He sat down next to an older lady who got up and moved to another seat farther back. He probably looked like he had something contagious.

When he reached his stop, he pulled himself from his seat with great difficulty and lurched toward the door. He stumbled stepping down and fell onto the pavement. The fall should have hurt, but his arms and legs felt nothing. The absence of pain was more frightening than normal pain would have been.

"Are you okay, buddy?" the bus driver asked.

Stanley nodded and lifted his numb right arm to wave him off. He knew he wasn't okay, but it wasn't like the bus driver could help him. He didn't even know if a doctor could help him at this point. He was pretty sure the antibiotics weren't going to do the trick. He grabbed the bus stop signpost and used it to pull himself up to a standing position. He was unsteady on both of his feet. He reached down and slapped his left leg. He felt nothing. He should have told the nurse in the walk-in clinic about the numbness in his limbs. What had he been thinking?

He staggered and stumbled down the sidewalk. Passersby stared, some seeming worried, others just annoyed, like it inconvenienced them to see another person suffering. He made his way into the storage yard and held on to stacks of lumber for support as he tried to propel himself toward the stairs that led down to the facility. He grabbed the stair railing with both hands and focused on taking one painstaking step down at a time. His progress was too slow, and he was afraid of clocking in late, so he finally sat down on a step and scooted down on his bottom, step by step, like his nephew when he was a toddler and scared of the stairs. It wasn't dignified, but it got him where he needed to go.

He passed the stinking biowaste bin. At least his nose still worked. That was something, anyway.

By the time he scanned his ID badge and the groaning door opened, Stanley was so exhausted it took all of his concentration to simply put one foot in front of the other. He had thought he might go to the storage room to find a fresh shirt, but looking professional no longer felt like a priority. Rest. That was his only priority. He dragged himself to the security office, scanned his ID badge, and collapsed into his chair, panting like a sick dog and sweating profusely.

He was in no condition to be at work. He was in no condition, period.

Looking down, he saw that his right leg and left leg were now equally swollen, stretching the fabric of his pants so tight it was in danger of ripping. Everything felt tight. His swollen arms, his swollen legs. Even his chest felt tight. Was this what it felt like to have a heart attack? Could he be having a heart attack? He would call Melissa in the morning and tell her to go ahead and make that doctor's appointment. No more messing around with walk-in clinics and antibiotics. This was serious, and now he was less scared of doctors than he was of this illness.

Amber. He kept thinking of Amber. When she broke up with him, he had just stared at her stupidly, too much in shock to say much of anything. There was so much he could have said to her, so much he needed to say. What if he never got the chance to say it?

With shaky, sweaty hands, he dug through his desk and found a pen and paper. From some emergency reserve of energy deep within himself, he wrote:

Dear Amber,

With his numb arm and his unsteady hand, the words looked like they had been written by a second grader. But he couldn't let that stop him. He kept on writing.

Do you remember how we first met in the grocery store? I brought my stuff to your register. You checked me out, and all that time I was checking you out. I was too nervous to ask you on a date, but I kept coming to the store and buying things I didn't need just so I could see you. Finally you said, "Do you like me or something?" I think I blushed, but I said yes, and you said, "Then why don't you ask me out?" When I did and you said yes, I think it was the happiest I have ever been. Amber, I know I wasn't always the best or most exciting boyfriend, but I want you to know that I truly loved you and still do. I have been real sick lately, and if you're reading this it's probably because something bad has happened to me. Please don't feel sad for me. I just want you to know I'm sorry I didn't make you happier and give you what you needed, but it wasn't because I didn't love you. I do and very much. I wish you lots of happiness in your life, as much happiness as you brought me when we were together.

Love always,

Stanley

There. That was it. He was no poet, and his handwriting looked terrible, but he had said what he needed to say. Trembling and exhausted, he folded up the letter and put it in his pocket for safekeeping. When he leaned back in his chair and closed his eyes, he didn't doze off as usual. Instead, he passed out as if somebody had hit him in the head with a baseball bat.

When he regained consciousness, he felt shaky and sweaty. And tight. *Tight* is the only way he could think to describe it, like somehow his body had been stretched to its limit. His pants were stretched snug across his legs, and now his T-shirt, roomy when he had put it on just a few hours before, clung to his every bulge and contour. But it wasn't just the clothing that was tight. His skin felt tight, too, as if it might burst open like the peel of an overripe fruit.

The ballerina doll was on the desk. He was in no mood to play. He didn't pick it up. He didn't even want to touch it.

"I like being close to you," it said.

"Sure you do," he mumbled, but then he thought, *Wait.* He put his face in his hands and tried to make some sense of his confused mind. *Doesn't the doll only talk when you tilt it over? Before, it only talked when I tilted it over. Maybe I didn't really hear that. Maybe I'm so sick I'm hallucinating.*

"Take me home with you," it said.

Stanley knew he heard it that time, but he didn't answer. One of his many recent problems was his tendency to talk to inanimate objects. Melissa was right. He needed to get out more; all this solitude wasn't good for him. He was already worried about his physical health. He didn't want to have to worry about his mental health, too.

But why was the doll talking if no one was activating it? Maybe it was broken; maybe there was some problem with the mechanism that caused the voice activation to shut off. Whatever the cause was, Stanley didn't like the effect.

"We like you," it said with that same little giggle that he had once found charming.

With a shaking hand, Stanley picked up the doll to

inspect it. Maybe there was a switch he hadn't noticed before that controlled the voice mechanism. Maybe he could turn the thing off.

The doll was missing an arm. Strange. It had been intact the night before. "What happened to your arm?" Stanley asked.

"Take me home with you," the one-armed doll said.

"No." He had said he wasn't going to talk to the doll anymore, so why was he doing it?

For some reason, the doll didn't seem so cute anymore. He couldn't say why, but the thought of having it in his apartment was terrifying. He wasn't so crazy about having it here, either.

Stanley remembered that when he had handled the doll the night before, he had noticed a tiny scratch in the paint job on its face. Tonight, the scratch wasn't there. Another night, he remembered now, he had noticed that there had been a small tear in the doll's tutu. Tonight, as it had been last night, the tutu was fine.

We like you.

We.

Suddenly Stanley understood. It hadn't been the same doll on his desk each night. It had been a different doll every time. Sure, it had been the same *type* of doll, but there had always been slight differences.

But what did it mean? Whatever it was, it was weird and upsetting, and he didn't want any part in it. He opened a drawer in the desk, dropped the one-armed doll inside it, and slammed the drawer shut. There. Out of sight, out of mind.

After he saw the doctor and got whatever these health issues were straightened out, Stanley decided he was going to look for a new job like Melissa was always encouraging him to do. She said they were always looking for good security guards over at the courthouse where she worked. That way, he could work in the daytime and actually see people and talk to them. Maybe he and Melissa could take their lunch breaks together sometimes. If he worked days, his schedule wouldn't be the opposite of all his buddies' anymore, and maybe he could start hanging out with the guys again. He could invite them over to his apartment, which he would keep scrupulously clean, and they could order pizza and watch football together.

Who knows? He might even start dating again. He would start by asking Katie out. Even if she turned him down, asking her would be good practice, a step in the right direction.

As soon as he got his health back, a job at the courthouse could be the solution to all his problems. It would be a sunny, sociable workplace—not like this one, all dark and creepy and lonely. Stanley thought about the future and felt a small sense of hope.

He told himself he wasn't going to fall asleep again. He was going to do his job. The screens were called monitors because he was supposed to monitor them. But his body, for whatever bizarre medical reason, was stretched beyond its limits, and exhaustion overtook him. His head lolled back as he slumped in the chair, and his eyes shut. He descended into blackness.

He was in a dentist's chair. The dental assistant was a robot outfitted as a ballerina. Unlike the little doll's, her face was painted to look feminine and pretty, with long eyelashes, pink lips, and pink circles on her cheeks. Her blue metal "hair" was sculpted into a ballet bun. She hovered over him, holding what looked like several wide belts. "We have to strap you in," she said, her voice feminine and sultry. "The doctor doesn't like squirming." She bound Stanley to the chair with leather straps around his shoulders, his arms, his legs. He wanted to move, wanted to fight being restrained, but he could not will his body to act. He was paralyzed.

The dentist entered wearing dark safety goggles and a surgical mask. Stanley was leaned back, his mouth open, his hands in a white-knuckled grip on the chair's armrests. The dentist was silent and rough and was trying to stretch Stanley's mouth to open wider and wider. No, *Stanley was saying in his head.* Stop! It won't open that wide! It can't! *The dentist reached up and tore off the goggles and the mask. The face Stanley saw was a clown-white mask with big black eyeholes and a black gaping grin. Yellow glowing irises shined through the black eye sockets. The face. He knew that face . . . the thing's hands pushed his mouth open even wider, wider than he could stand. His lips were going to split at the corners, his jaw was going to break . . .*

Stanley woke up, but the feeling of stretching didn't stop.

That face in the dream. Stanley knew that face. It was . . .

Stanley was distracted from his thoughts by a sensation on his own face. There was something moving on his face.

The ballerina doll was standing on his chin, using her one arm and one of her legs to try to stretch his mouth open wide enough . . . wide enough for what?

Stanley's heart raced as he finally understood. *Wide enough so she could fit inside.*

Stanley raised his numb right arm and swatted the doll away. She was light and sailed across the room, hitting the wall with a thud and landing in a crumpled heap on the floor. He braced his hands on the desk to pull himself to his feet. As he stood, he felt a tightening in his arms, his legs, his belly, his chest. He knew now that what he was feeling was the sensation of dozens of tiny limbs pressing on his skin from the inside. Inside his arms, his legs, his chest, his belly—how many of them were in there?

The sore throat had started after the night the first doll appeared.

No wonder it hurt too much to eat or drink anything. Night after night, the dolls had been climbing into his mouth and down his throat as he slept, making their way through the narrow passageways of his body like explorers in a dark, damp cave. The realization nauseated him. He felt the urge to vomit, but there was nothing in his stomach to bring up. Nothing but acid and fear.

He wished he could go back to not knowing what was

wrong with him, to just thinking he had contracted some unusual virus or infection. People always said that when it came to physical conditions, knowing was better than not knowing. In this case, they were wrong. Knowing was much, much worse.

Stanley staggered out of the office and down the hall. Everything in his head screamed at him to run, but he was too weak to run. The walls of the facility seemed to be closing in around him. He had never liked this place. He had to get out of here for good, he told himself, and he would do it even if he had to crawl. The pressure inside him was building. It felt like the dolls were angry, like their many tiny fists were punching him and their many tiny feet were kicking him. But he saw the EXIT sign's green glow up ahead. Green means go, he told himself. If he could just get out, if he could be where there was moonlight and fresh air to breathe, he could figure out what to do. He leaned against the wall and hobbled to the EXIT sign.

Outside, he tried to take a breath of fresh air but instead sucked in the stench from the biowaste bin. He was so worn out and ill that he wanted to just lie down on the pavement, but he had to figure out a way to make it up the stairs. Up the stairs and into a cab and straight to the emergency room, where he would tell them—what? *There are dozens of little dolls living inside me. They crawl down my throat when I sleep.* There was no doubt what ward of the hospital a statement like that would land him in. But maybe if he could convince a doctor to take an X-ray, they could see that the dolls were real . . .

Voices. Stanley's thoughts were interrupted by tiny, muffled little-girlish voices. They were muffled because they were coming from inside him.

From his left arm: *"I like being close to you."*

From his right leg: *"We like you."*

From his belly: *"You're so warm and squishy."*

Stanley stumbled backward, almost falling. Standing was becoming more and more difficult. The pressure was building inside him, becoming unbearable. He felt like he might explode. Could that happen? Could a person actually explode?

The tiny one-armed doll was standing framed in the facility's doorway, posed like she was about to do a pirouette. The yellow irises of her cavernous black eyes focused on Stanley like lasers. Her smile was wide. She tilted her head in a way that under other circumstances might have been cute. "Isn't there room for just one more?" she chirped.

All of Stanley's strength was gone. He fell to his knees. The one-armed doll leaped toward him with the grace of a ballerina.

Stanley couldn't help it. He opened his mouth to scream.

THE NEW KID

It's a bright, sunny day, the kind of day that makes you feel like you have to do something. You have to do something fun, or you have to 'be productive.'" Devon used his left index and middle fingers to make air quotes, trusting no one would notice his chewed-on cuticles and bitten-down nails. Then he continued in what he hoped was an ominous tone, "It's the kind of day when your mom makes you mow the lawn. But today isn't a mowing day. Today is a birthday party day."

Devon heard rustling in the classroom. Someone snickered, but he didn't look up from his papers. He kept his head bent, his long hair hanging like a protective shield between him and the class.

Normally, he hated having to stand in front of the class . . . for any reason, but today he was on a mission. If he had to read a stupid assignment for English class, he was going to make it work for him.

Devon continued with his story, describing the birthday party scene for a pack of screaming four-year-olds. He read about the balloons and the clowns and the bright-colored bounce house set up in the middle of the green lawn.

"But this isn't any ordinary bounce house," Devon read. "No one knows that yet, but they're going to find out . . . now." Devon paused for effect. He didn't hear anything. For all he knew, his teacher, Mrs. Patterson, and his classmates had disappeared. But he wasn't going to look up to see.

Devon went on, "Because now little Halley is crawling into the bounce house. She's the first one in. Her twin sister, Hope, is right behind her."

Was that a gasp Devon heard from the third row of desks? He thought it was. Good. He had her attention. He grinned as he kept reading. "Halley makes it almost all the way into the bounce house, her bright pink dress clashing with the house's puffy red vinyl floor. 'Faster,' Hope urges Halley, pushing Halley's butt. Halley still crawls slowly, until suddenly, she's sucked inside the bounce house. Hope giggles and follows her."

Devon stopped reading again. He was getting to the good part. "But in a second, Hope is going to wish she didn't follow her sister. In just a second, she's looking down as she crawls inside, but now, she's in. She looks up and she sees her sister's partially eaten body lying still on the red vinyl. No wait! The vinyl isn't red. It's covered in blood." Was that a squeal Devon just heard? He kept reading, "And the house isn't a house. It's a big mouth, and the mouth is chewing, and now it's opening wider, and Hope, now screaming, is sliding into—"

"That's enough!" Mrs. Patterson shouted.

Devon blinked. He still didn't look up. He wasn't finished.

"Devon Blaine Marks." Mrs. Patterson spurted every one of Devon's three names like each was a spitball. Before he could respond, Mrs. Patterson's large square hand appeared in front of Devon's downward-aimed gaze and snatched the story from his grasp. The pages rattled, and he felt the sting of a paper cut on the web of skin between his thumb and index finger.

The classroom was so silent Devon could hear a bird chirping outside the window. He finally looked up at Mrs. Patterson. "What?"

"What?" Mrs. Patterson shook her head, sending her blonde ponytail into a wild dance.

Mrs. Patterson was an English teacher, but she was also the girls' basketball coach. She was a huge woman, tall and broad in the shoulders. She towered over Devon, and Devon was already 5'9"—tall for his age. If only he were coordinated enough to be a basketball player. Maybe then he'd be a part of—

"Devon." Mrs. Patterson softened her deep voice, and Devon finally raised his gaze to look at her wide face. He even managed to meet her intense blue eyes. Mrs. Patterson's eyes were scary. Everyone in the class thought so. She could reduce you to a pile of smoke and ashes with just a look. Devon was happy he was still standing.

"Report to Mr. Wright's office," Mrs. Patterson ordered.

Devon looked at his story, crumpled in Mrs. Patterson's hand. He wanted to argue, but he shrugged and headed toward the classroom door.

Heather sat in the second seat from the door, in the third row. As he passed that row, he met her gaze. Had it worked?

Heather was looking right at him. Looking right at him! Yes!

Heather Anders, one of the most popular girls in his class, and by far the prettiest, had never, not one single time, ever, *ever* looked at Devon. As far as Heather, and pretty much all of their ninth-grade class, was concerned, Devon didn't exist. Or if she had noticed he existed, he was nothing more than part of the scenery, like a blackboard or a chair. If it wasn't for Devon's best, and only, friend, Mick, and his well-meaning but very annoying mom, Devon would wonder if he did, in fact, exist. Sometimes he wasn't so sure.

But today, he existed. And Heather saw him. Triumphant, he grinned at her and gave her a thumbs-up as he sauntered toward the classroom door.

Heather rolled her eyes and said, "Jeez, Devon. That was sick."

Devon grinned wider and stood tall as he nodded at her and then strode out of the classroom like he was heading to an important meeting instead of to the principal's office.

He'd done it.

Even though Heather never noticed Devon, he'd made a careful study of Heather. He watched her. He listened to her. He wanted to know everything about her.

The previous week, while Mick was going on about his latest superhero obsession, Devon was listening to Heather talk to her girlfriends. She was complaining about her four-year-old twin sisters, Halley and Hope. "They drive me crazy," she told Valerie, her best friend. "I mean seriously bonkers. I'm always having to babysit them, and I *hate it*. They're always getting into trouble, breaking something or whatever, and then *I* get in trouble. *I hate them!*"

That same day, Mrs. Patterson handed out the assignment to write an original short story. That's when Devon saw his chance. He saw it. He took it. And he'd made the most of it.

Who cared if it cost him a trip to the principal's office? The best creative artists had hidden depths lurking beneath the surface . . . and usually, those depths were misunderstood.

Devon and Mick met up after school at their regular spot in the back, at the edge of the teachers' parking lot. Devon couldn't wait to talk to Mick about what had happened with Heather. He hadn't thought to look at Mick before he left English class. He wasn't sure his friend saw what had happened. Mick tended to daydream. He was often caught staring out the school windows at who knew what.

When Devon reached Mick, Mick was juggling his bright purple backpack, a papier-mâché tiger, a plastic go-cup with a curlicue straw, a stack of books that obviously wouldn't fit in the overstuffed backpack, and a half-eaten package of chocolate cupcakes. White frosting from the missing cupcake was stuck to his lower lip.

Devon pointed at the frosting.

"Huh? What? Oh." Mick wiped at his mouth with the back of the hand holding the tiger. It made him look like he was being mauled. It also made him drop the stack of books, which smacked the ground and scattered.

Devon shook his head and bent over to pick them up. He stuck them in his own navy-blue backpack, which was nearly empty. He'd already done his homework for the day while he was hanging out in Mr. Wright's office, and unlike Mick, Devon never read a book he wasn't required to read.

"Sorry. Oh, you got those?" Mick asked. "Thanks." Mick squinted at Devon through his round wire-rimmed glasses. He shoved his reddish-blond bangs off his freckled forehead—they ended up sticking straight up. "Where's your art project?"

"I dumped it in the trash."

"Why? That four-headed octopus was gnarly."

Devon shrugged. He didn't tell Mick that he thought making papier-mâché animals was for kids, and that the art teacher, Mr. Steward, had given Devon a D on the project and a lecture on following instructions instead of doing whatever he wanted. "These were supposed to be representations of *real* animals, Mr. Marks," Mr. Steward had said.

"How do you know there aren't any four-headed octopuses?" Devon had responded. "Only five percent of the ocean floor has been explored."

That had shut Mr. Steward up.

Devon didn't like reading books, but that didn't mean he didn't read. He spent most of his spare time on the Internet.

Mick stuffed the second cupcake in his mouth. The boys started walking away from the school.

Mick took a noisy slurp through his straw. "That was a

skeevy short story, Dev. Kind of made me throw up in my mouth."

Devon gave Mick a gentle shove. "Gross."

"No grosser than your story."

"Whatever. Did you see what Heather did, though?"

"She was, like, really white, her face, I mean. I thought she was gonna faint."

"Yeah? But did you see her look at me?"

Mick glanced at Devon, who bent down to pick up a round stone. He flung it at a STOP sign, and it hit the middle of the O with a resounding metallic *clink*.

"Um, I saw her look at you like she wanted to kill you."

"Nah. Didn't you hear what she said?"

Mick adjusted his backpack. "Yep. She said the story was sick."

"No, she said it was 'sic,' as in cool."

Mick screwed up his round face. "Um, I don't think so."

Devon shrugged again, picked up another rock, and fired it at a lamppost. He got a resonant *bong* as a reward. "The point is that she noticed me. She talked to me."

Mick twisted his small mouth. "That's something?"

"It sure is!"

The boys had reached the railroad yard that was half a mile from their school. They began weaving through the stationary, graffiti-covered boxcars. The railway yard smelled like oil and creosote, and it was filled with the sounds of train wheels clunking lethargically over dirty old rails. At the far side of the yard, the boys ducked into the woods that stretched for miles to the north beyond the railroad yard and from several miles east of the yard to the back of their neighborhood to the west. The woods were thick with huge fir and hemlock trees that stood so closely together in places that they blocked out the sun, creating perpetual dusk. On a cloudy day, the forest was even darker, like it was one big shadow engulfing and muting the too-loud, too-bright, too-busy craziness that most people called real life. Devon loved the darkness, and on a sunny day like today, it was a relief to duck into the trees and leave the blazing light behind.

Halfway from the railroad yard to the neighborhood, if they stayed near the edge of the woods, they'd reach their "clubhouse," the hangout they had set up in an old abandoned gas station that backed onto the woods. For the six years they'd been friends, they'd spent nearly every afternoon after school and much of every weekend in their clubhouse.

If Devon was honest—which he wasn't—he thought they were getting a little old to have a clubhouse. It was fine when they were in grade school and maybe even last year in middle school, but now that they were nearly at the end of their freshman year, it was too "little kid" for them. Devon had outgrown their pretend games of pirates and space cowboys, and he no longer saw the collection of junk they'd amassed over the years as "treasures." He didn't want to be one of two boys who had no place to go after school other than a tumbling-down empty gas station. But that didn't mean he had a problem with their clubhouse. It might not be little-kid fun for him anymore, but it was a place to get away from all the crap of real life. It was a place he could go and forget about school and forget about all the pressure his mom was always putting on him to "be somebody."

"Don't end up like me, Devon. Be somebody," she told him over and over and over and—

"Don't you think?" Mick asked.

"What?" How long had he been walking along not listening to his friend? Devon had no idea what he'd missed, but he figured it probably wasn't important. Mick's latest favorite subject of conversation was the digital math game he was working on. "It's going to be like playing spy, like with ciphers," Mick had explained to Devon.

Mick and Devon got mostly *B*s and *C*s, peppered with the occasional *D*, at school. That wasn't, however, because they were stupid. They weren't. Devon just never cared enough about school to "apply himself"—his mother's words. School bored him. Why work hard at it? Mick's problem was a little more serious. He had some learning disorders Devon didn't really understand, and he tended to have attention issues. "We're not going to label the boy," Mick's father said (according to Mick), so Mick had never been treated for anything. Basically, as far as Devon could tell, Mick was a like a savant who couldn't figure out how to play the school game. And Mick didn't care about the school game. He was in love with food (the reason for his soft, slightly pudgy form) and fantasy worlds of any kind. Mick was an overgrown kid, almost as tall as Devon. Mick's high-waisted corduroy pants and button-down short-sleeve shirts screamed "nerd," but it didn't seem to bother him. Devon figured someday Mick would probably own a gaming company and be a zillionaire.

"Devon!" Mick yanked on Devon's T-shirt sleeve.

"What?" Mick blinked and looked around. They should be at the clubhouse by now. Yep, there was the old cedar tree with the split trunk, so . . .

Where was the gas station?

"It's gone," Mick said in a very small voice.

He was right. The gas station was no longer there. In its place, a hulking yellow backhoe sat idle next to a mass of debris like a dragon waiting to spew fire at its defeated foe.

Mick plopped down on a fallen log. "But . . ." He blinked and sniffed. "Our treasures."

Devon, who was feeling strangely thrilled by the demolished clubhouse, looked down at his friend. Mick's large brown eyes were moist. He rubbed his nose.

Devon took a seat next to Mick and threw an arm around his shoulders. "Hey, it's okay."

"But it's not! Look!"

"Yeah, I'm looking."

"All our treasures," Mick repeated.

"Yeah. But we can find more." Not that Devon wanted to, but Mick didn't need to know that.

"But, we have no clubhouse now!"

Devon gave Mick a half hug, glad no one could see them. "I'll find us something."

"You think so?"

"Sure. And in the meantime, we have the forest." He waved an arm behind them.

"Well, yeah, that'll work on days like today, but—"

"Leave it to me," Devon said. "For now, let's just hang out here. No matter what, we're in it together, right?" He held out his right index finger.

Mick grinned and nodded. "In it together." He extended his right index finger and linked it with Devon's. They both pulled hard and then released.

Devon shrugged out of his backpack and unzipped the outer pocket. "I saved the chocolate chip cookie from my lunch. It's yours if you want it."

Mick brightened. "Really? Far out."

Devon inwardly rolled his eyes. He was used to Mick's habit of using out-of-date or even made-up slang, but that didn't mean he always liked it.

While Mick munched on the cookie, Devon said, "I think today's a big day. Maybe that"—he waved at the pile of destroyed gas station—"is a sign that something new is coming, something big. I mean, after all, Heather *talked* to me today. All I have to do now is build on that and figure out other ways to get her attention."

Mick stopped chewing. He brushed cookie crumbs off his chin. "Um . . . I'm not sure getting her attention is necessarily a good thing. There are different kinds of attention, right?"

Devon shrugged. "Whatever." Devon was happy with how his plan unfolded today; he wasn't going to let Mick talk him off his high. "Hey," he said, "why don't we go poke around that pile and see if we can find some of our stuff?"

Mick, who had finished the cookie, grinned.

Mrs. Patterson seemed to be bearing a grudge about Devon's story. Instead of ignoring him like normal, she glared at him as he took his usual place in the back of the room next to Mick. Heather wasn't here yet.

As soon as Devon sat down, Mick leaned over and poked him in the arm. "Hey, Dev, you need to meet Kelsey." Mick leaned back and pointed at a new kid sitting on Mick's left. "Kelsey, this is Devon. Dev, this is Kelsey."

"Hey," Kelsey said. He flashed Devon what looked like a genuine, friendly smile.

Really?

Devon had spotted Kelsey earlier that morning. He'd been hanging out near the stairs watching the other kids. Both then and now, Devon thought Kelsey didn't look like the kind of kid who would be friendly with Mick and Devon. Although Devon didn't dress with nerdy abandon like Mick did, he in no way resembled a normal kid. Too skinny for his height, Devon knew he had a lot of things working against him: his teeth were super crooked and his mom couldn't afford to get him braces; his ears were too big—even though he wore his dark hair long and as messy as possible, the ears still wanted to stick out; his neck was too long; and his dark eyes were way too small and way too close together. When he was in grade school, one of the school bullies called him "Birdman." His mom liked to say he was a "dormant swan." Yeah, whatever.

But here was this new kid, this very good-looking (Devon knew what girls looked for in boys) new kid, smiling at Devon as if Devon were someone worth smiling at. Devon had seen Kelsey smile at lots of kids the same way when he was on the stairs.

Kelsey's smile made Devon feel ridiculously good.

"Kelsey just moved here," Mick said.

Devon resisted the urge to say, "Duh."

"His dad's a contractor," Mick continued. "He's here to head up that hotel/office complex my dad bid on and didn't get." His grin and bright eyes made it clear he didn't intend any spite in these words. Even so, Devon noticed Kelsey's smile faltered for a second.

Devon had no idea what to say to that, so he just said, "Okay." It was bad enough that Mick had just mentioned his often-out-of-work dad, who liked to grouse about how other electricians were always outbidding him. But Devon hoped this conversation wasn't going to end up with him having to say what his mom did. She was a house cleaner. She didn't even have her own housecleaning business. She worked for someone else. She barely made enough money for them to live on, but she seemed to think he should be proud that they were "making it." He wasn't.

"I invited Kelsey to sit with us at lunch," Mick said.

"Sure," Devon said, not at all sure Kelsey would actually *want* to sit with them.

Kelsey grinned. "I appreciate the invite."

Devon raised an eyebrow and scanned Kelsey's wavy blond hair, blue eyes, straight teeth, broad shoulders, cool ripped jeans, and faded black T-shirt. "Sure," he repeated.

The disjointed sound of multiple conversations, the swish of clothes, the scraping of chairs, and the thudding of books on desks let Devon know the classroom was filling up. He got a whiff of Heather's lemony scent, and he swiveled in his seat to stare at the sleek shine of her straight auburn hair. She was wearing a dark-green shirt that went great with her hair.

"Okay, cease and desist with the chaos," Mrs. Patterson said. "Let's begin."

To Devon's shock, Kelsey did actually sit with Mick and him during lunch. It was another bright day, and everyone was outside either clustered at the picnic tables set up near the entrance to the cafeteria or lounging on the grass that stretched from the walkway in front of the school to the parking lot. Devon and Mick leaned against the base of the stone wall surrounding the flag posts.

The stone was rough but warm. Devon was looking for Heather, and Mick was going on about how *delicious* peanut butter and honey sandwiches were, when Kelsey strolled over and dropped to a cross-legged position in front of them.

Devon glanced up and around them to see if anyone was looking at this shocking social development. Several people were. A couple of the jocks called out, "Hey, Kelsey" as they strutted past. Kelsey smiled at them. "Hey, Kurt. Hey, Brian." He also waved at a group of girls at the closest picnic table, and they waved back. Then he turned his attention to Mick and Devon.

"I hear the food sucks here, so I brought my own lunch," he said.

Mick waved around his "delicious" sandwich and said in peanut-butter-mush-mouth, "Ish the besht chose."

Kelsey laughed. He actually laughed, not like as if he was laughing at Mick, but like he thought Mick was amusing. He opened a crumpled brown-paper bag. "I like good old chicken salad," he said. "My mom makes great chicken salad." He gestured at Devon's sack. "What do you have?"

Devon shrugged. "I'm not actually hungry." He pushed his sack down into his backpack. The truth was he had bologna on white bread. His mom bought both in bulk. And he hated both. He hated the taste, and he hated that they reminded him of grade school, when he'd thought bologna was the best thing in the world.

He'd outgrown the food, but their budget hadn't kept up with his taste buds.

Kelsey bit into his sandwich and looked around. "I like it here. I like the sun."

"See, Dev? Normal people like the sun." Mick nudged Devon with a foot and said to Kelsey, "Dev likes clouds. If I didn't know better, I'd think he was a vampire."

Kelsey tilted his head and studied Devon for a couple seconds. For those two seconds, Devon had the weird feeling he was being evaluated. But then Kelsey laughed and leaned toward Devon. "Well, he doesn't sparkle in the sun like those movie vampires." He laughed again. "Probably not a vampire."

Devon said in creepy vampire accent, "I don't vant to suck your blood."

"Hey, Kelsey," a girl's bell-like voice called out.

Devon sat up straight. It was Heather.

"Hi, Heather," Kelsey said. "You find that book I was telling you about?"

She stood a few feet from them and beamed down at Kelsey. "I did. I'm going to start it tonight." She flicked a glance at Mick and Devon. "Oh, hi, Devon."

The tone of Heather's voice when she said hi to Devon was totally different than the one she used for Kelsey. Devon noticed that, of course. Part of his brain told him that the sharp and heavy tones on each syllable of his name represented sarcasm. Part of his brain didn't care; it only cared that she said hi to him.

"Hi, Heather."

She wrinkled her nose at him, flashed a big smile at Kelsey, and walked away.

"Pretty girl," Kelsey said softly after Heather had moved off. He watched her for a few seconds, then scanned the rest of the students, his gaze resting now and then on someone before moving on.

"Yeah," Mick said. "Devon thinks—"

"Yes, she is," Devon interrupted. He turned and gave Mick a look that clearly said "Shut up." Mick was sharp enough to quietly return to his sandwich.

Kelsey started talking about the experiment they'd done in science class, and Devon tuned out. He watched Heather talking animatedly with her friends while he half listened to Kelsey and Mick discuss chemical reagents. Was this what it was like to actually fit in? Maybe not quite, but it was closer then he'd gotten in years.

Devon pretty much floated through the rest of the day. He hadn't felt this good in a very long time. He even raised his hand once in math and answered a question correctly. Mr. Crenshaw's mouth dropped open.

On his way through the school to meet Mick after his last class, Devon passed Heather and her friends loitering by the lockers. Heather stood with her back to the hallway. Her friends formed a semicircle in front of her. There was Valerie and Juliet, along with her third BFF, Gabriella.

Gabriella's boyfriend, Quincy, also stood nearby; for some reason Devon didn't understand, Quincy always seemed to be hanging out with the three girls.

"I've decided I'm going to make my own movies." Heather flung her hair back over her shoulder. "I don't want to be an actress. I want to be behind the camera."

Devon didn't think. He just stopped next to Heather and started talking. Ignoring Heather's friends, he pushed in sideways in front of Heather and said, "If you're going to make movies, you should do horror movies. Even campy horror movies can get good followings."

Heather took a step back and looked Devon up and down.

He kept talking. "If you decide to do horror movies, let me know. I have a cousin who has clown makeup and costumes. You could do a creepy-clown story."

Heather tapped a red-nailed index finger against Devon's chest. Emphasizing each word with what could have been scorn . . . but maybe not, she pronounced, "You are unoriginal. That's been done, done, done." She turned and flounced off. Her friends followed but not before Valerie, her blonde curls bouncing as she shook her head at Devon, said, "You are very weird."

Devon watched them walk away as he rubbed the spot Heather touched. She touched him!

As Mick and Devon headed away from school, Mick waited for Devon to talk about his search for a new clubhouse, but Devon didn't talk about that.

"She actually touched me!" Devon was saying. He'd just finished telling Mick how he'd talked to Heather in the hall. It sounded to Mick like Devon had made himself look like a total doofus, but Devon didn't see it that way. Devon actually thought Heather's comment and her fingertip to the chest were worth getting excited about.

Mick was a little worried about Devon. It seemed like he was getting just a bit delusional.

It wasn't that Mick thought Devon didn't deserve to get Heather's attention. Sure he did. Mick's parents had taught him that looks don't mean anything, and everyone is equally deserving of love and other good stuff. Mick had to admit he wasn't really sure the world worked that way. He hadn't seen evidence of this attitude in school, for sure, but he trusted his parents.

A bee buzzed past Mick's nose, and he jumped back and waved his go-cup in front of his face. The liquid inside sloshed around. He watched Devon throw a rock at the coupling on the end of one of the boxcars. He hit it dead-on.

But he was missing big-time with his conclusions about Heather. Devon's latest conversational attempt was a swing and a very, very big miss.

Mick grinned. His dad would be proud of the sports metaphor. Mick hadn't liked sports when he was younger, but lately he'd been getting into baseball, which his dad loved. Mick liked the stats.

As Mick and Devon ducked into the woods, Mick said, "Uh, Dev? What's going on with looking for a new clubhouse?"

"Huh?" Devon had been talking about Heather's hair. He blinked and looked at Mick.

"A new clubhouse?" Mick repeated.

"Oh, right. I'm still looking for something good, but in the meantime, I stashed a blanket, a tarp, and some ropes in the woods early this morning. I thought we could build a fort and make it like our camp."

Mick grinned. "Badonkadonk! That's the boss."

Mick noticed Devon sigh. He knew Devon didn't like his expressions, but he didn't care. They made Mick happy, and Mick liked to do whatever he could to be happy. He was pretty sure Devon thought Mick didn't care about fitting in at school. But Mick *did* care. He cared so much it actually hurt him to think about how much everyone ignored them both, but the alternative—putting themselves out there and being rejected—was decidedly something Mick didn't want. He and Devon both used to deal with it in the same way—by ignoring everyone else and doing their own thing. Now Devon seemed to want to try to fit in, while Mick still wanted to try to stay in his fantasy world. The fantasy world felt good. The real world definitely did not.

A few minutes later, they reached a small stand of

hemlocks sheltering a couple of boulders. Devon went to one of the boulders and pulled out a blanket, a tarp, and some rope. Between the two of them, they managed to string up the tarp to form a lopsided and sagging roof, and they spread the blanket on the ground between the boulders.

"So let's brainstorm," Dev said when they'd settled, and Mick had offered him a barbecue potato chip from the bag he bought from the vending machine after school. Every day, his mom gave him money to get some kind of junk food from that machine. It was his reward for getting through another day. Some days he got something sugary, and when he did, he usually ate it immediately. Some days he got something salty, and he usually saved that to share with Devon.

"About the clubhouse?" Mick asked. "Is that what we're brainstorming?"

Devon crunched a chip and said, "What? No. About Heather and how I can get in with her more."

"Um? Dude, I'm still not sure you're getting in with her *yet*."

Devon ignored Mick. "I need to find a way to impress her," he said.

"That's never a good idea," Mick said.

"What isn't?"

"Doing something to try to impress someone. My mom says that's when boys make stupid mistakes."

Devon flicked a rock at a fern growing at the base of

one of the trees holding up their tarp. "Well, who cares what your mom says?"

"Um? I do?"

"Yeah, well, you shouldn't."

"How about we talk about the hike we're going to do on Saturday?" Mick asked. "Dad says if we go a couple miles farther north than we normally go, we'll find a pretty jiggy waterfall."

"Maybe we should scout out locations for her movies," Devon said. "I could give her a list of good locations. That should make her happy."

"Apparently there's some kind of rare plant that grows next to the waterfall," Mick tried again. "It would be cool beans to find it."

"Why would Heather want beans?" Devon said.

Mick laughed, but then he realized Devon was serious. He hadn't been listening to anything Mick said. Mick sighed. It was like Devon had been put under a witch's spell. Mick wondered how he could break it.

To Devon's amazement, Kelsey met Devon and Mick for lunch again the next day. He even brought his new friends chicken salad sandwiches. "I thought you'd like to try them," Kelsey said. "Mom makes her own bread, too. It's pretty awesome."

Today, the weather was more to Devon's liking. So many cloud tufts clustered overhead they blocked out most of the sun.

"Hey," Kelsey said, jerking his thumb toward the sky. "Your kind of weather."

He remembered that? Devon smiled. "Yeah."

Devon had watched Kelsey in the two classes they shared. It seemed like Kelsey was making friends with every kid in the class. How did he do that?

Was it just because he was good-looking? Was it the clothes? Today, he wore baggy black pants with a gray T-shirt. He had a black-and-red plaid shirt tied at his waist. Devon had never cared about clothes enough to know what was right and what was wrong to wear. There was no reason to care. His mom could afford to get him two pairs of jeans and a bunch of T-shirts every year. That limited his fashion choices.

"So do you know all the cloud types?" Kelsey asked. "We learned them in school last year, and the only one I can remember is stratus. What're those?" He gestured overhead.

"Cumulus," Devon said without thinking.

Maybe that was it. Kelsey talked to you like he actually cared about what you were into. Did he really care, or was it an act? Devon narrowed his eyes and studied Kelsey as Kelsey asked Mick about Mick's superhero watch. "I saw that latest movie," Kelsey said. "It was dope."

Kelsey was starting to get on Devon's nerves.

Wait a minute. What? Why? Devon frowned. Why was Kelsey bugging him? He should be glad the new kid was hanging with them. He *was* glad. But he was annoyed, too. It just came so easily to Kelsey. Too easily. It wasn't fair.

Devon snorted.

Mick and Kelsey looked at him. "What?" Mick said.

"Oh, sorry. Just had a stupid thought. Not important."

Kelsey cocked his head and looked at Devon so hard it felt like Kelsey was looking into his soul. Then Kelsey grinned and nodded as if he understood exactly. But how could he?

"Don't you just hate it when you brain goes and comes up with stupid thoughts? Mine does that all the time," Kelsey said. "It's like it has a mind of its own." He laughed.

Mick laughed, too. "Brain has a mind of its own. That's a good one."

Devon forced a chuckle. "Yeah, ha, ha."

He actually had been laughing at himself because he'd sounded like a baby when he thought it wasn't fair. As if. By now, he of all people should know life wasn't fair.

"What do you guys do after school?" Kelsey asked. "I've been looking into what's available and haven't decided what to get into yet."

Devon didn't want to answer that question. He and Mick weren't involved in any sports or clubs . . . except their "club" of two. They had nothing.

Mick wasn't intimidated by the question. With naïve honesty, he said, "We had this clubhouse, this really cool hangout in an abandoned gas station, but they tore it down. Dev said he's going to look for a new place for us."

Kelsey finished his sandwich and wiped his mouth with a black napkin. Who used black napkins?

"A hangout?" He leaned forward. "Well, you know, the best places for hangouts are abandoned buildings. My friends and I at my last school really got into urban exploring. We found some cool spots. When I learned I was coming here, I asked one of my buddies to let me know if there's anything around here worth checking out. He's looking into it."

"Cool," Mick said.

"But until then, I can still help with the hangout thing."

"You can?" Mick finished his sandwich, too, but didn't wipe off the chicken salad smeared on his cheek.

Kelsey pointed at it, and without making fun, he said, "You got a little smudge there."

"Oh. Thanks." Mick wiped his face with the back of his hand.

Kelsey smiled. "My parents bought this huge old farmhouse right outside of town. Mom says it's historical or something. I don't care about that, but I do like that there's this big old workshop behind the house. It's a mess, like sagging and starting to fall apart, and it needs paint and a new roof and stuff. Dad's building a home office and shop on the other side of the house, so he said I could have the workshop for a hangout place for parties and whatever if I fix it up. Want to help me? Dad said he'd buy all the supplies. I just have to do the work. He's taught me so I know how to build things. But it's more fun with friends. We could redo the workshop and make it our hangout."

Did he really just say "it's more fun with friends"? Devon was tempted to stab Kelsey and see if he was a robot. Kids just didn't say stuff like that.

Mick didn't seem to have a problem with it. He was practically bouncing. "That's the bee's knees!"

Kelsey laughed. "Glad you think so." He grinned at Devon. "How about you?"

"Knees," Devon said as dryly as possible. But he smiled. "That does sound pretty great."

And it did. Even though he resented how easily Kelsey was sliding into their class, he had to admit it would be awesome if being friends with Kelsey got them a ticket to the inner circle. If they helped build the hangout and Kelsey had parties, they'd be invited.

"Great," Kelsey said. He pulled out his phone and sent a text. "There's this old guy, George, a neighbor I've made friends with. I just texted him to see if he can take us to the building supply store after school tomorrow. He told me he could drive me whenever I needed it."

A couple seconds later, Kelsey's phone played a guitar riff. He glanced at it. "Yep, he's in." He glanced at his watch and stood.

Mick and Devon stood, too. It was time to get to class.

"Meet us tomorrow after school by the flag poles," Kelsey said. "Dad has a big dually pickup truck with an extra cab. Plenty of room for us all. It's bright red. You won't be able to miss it."

"Capital, my man!" Mick said in a fake British accent.

Kelsey laughed and offered Mick a fist to bump. "Jolly good," he played along. He offered his fist to Devon, too. Devon bumped it and said, "See ya" as they went into the school.

He noticed and ignored the flutter in his belly as he got his books from his locker. He was excited about Kelsey's offer, but he wasn't sure it was a good idea to get too revved up about it. Life had a way of disappointing him.

Maybe things were going to turn around, though. As Heather swished past and gave him a chilly stare, he let himself believe in the possibility of change.

Mick was so hyped up he could barely sit still. He hadn't been able to sleep the night before because he was too excited about helping Kelsey build the new clubhouse. Or, okay, *hangout*. Clubhouse. Hangout. Whatever.

His mom had noticed Mick had dark circles under his eyes when he got up, so she'd let him have a cup of coffee. Now he was on a caffeine high. He'd talked Devon's ear off on the way to school, and in every class, his leg had bounced like a basketball dribbled by a pro. Whoa. There was another sports metaphor, and he didn't even like basketball. How about that?

It was the third period of the day. They were in social studies. Not his favorite class, but he'd endure.

As usual, Mick and Devon sat in the back of the classroom with the map-lined walls and the stern Mr. Gentry looming over the kids in the front row. Mick noticed Kelsey was at the end of the third row sitting next to a couple of football players. Kelsey was leaning back in his chair sideways, so he was looking at the kids on the left side of the room instead of at Mr. Gentry up front. Mick watched as Kelsey's gaze landed on Devon and Mick. Kelsey gave them a little half smile and nodded.

"Today," Mr. Gentry said, "we're talking about justice." He peered over his black thick-rimmed reading glasses, which generally hung on the end of his beaky nose.

Mick thought Mr. Gentry looked a little like an eagle. He had white hair, and he usually wore brown. He had close-set eyes like Devon did. And then there was that nose.

"What is justice?" Mr. Gentry asked.

No one raised their hands.

I know a rhetorical question when I hear one, Mick thought.

"Every culture has its own concept of justice," Mr. Gentry continued. "This concept is generally derived from many fields of study. Our system of justice, for example, comes from ethics, rational thought, the law, religion, and just general ideas about fairness. Underlying all of that, though, is usually some kind of gut feeling. Justice is, in most cases, intuitive. We know it when we feel it." He looked out over the class. "So what does justice mean to you?"

This wasn't a rhetorical question. Mick didn't even think about raising his hand, though. Raising his hand in class would require that he have a brain transplant or maybe get possessed or be infected by an alien symbiont.

Kelsey raised his hand and said, "Justice balances the scales."

"What does that mean?" Mr. Gentry asked.

"It removes the downside so the downside can't outweigh the upside."

"Interesting perspective," Mr. Gentry said.

Heather raised her hand.

Mick frowned.

Heather.

What was it about Heather that fascinated Devon so much?

Sure, she was pretty, but she seemed pretty shallow to Mick. And she wasn't *that* pretty. There were much prettier girls in the class. He thought Devon was a little *cuhrazy* about Heather, though Devon seemed a little scrambled in general. Mick was beginning to think maybe *Devon* had picked up a symbiont. There was something in his eyes, something not quite . . . right.

"I think justice is payback," Heather said.

"Payback," Mr. Gentry repeated.

"Yeah," Heather said. "Like someone disses you, so you have to diss them back."

"'Payback' seems a little vague," Mr. Gentry said. "Perhaps it's too open to interpretation. What if payback goes too far?"

Heather shrugged. "Accidents happen." She laughed, and the class laughed with her. Devon laughed the loudest.

Mick noticed Kelsey wasn't laughing. Mick wasn't laughing, either. A shiver slithered down his spine.

Devon didn't think the day would ever end. Every class was slow and boring, with social studies winning the prize. Except for Heather's hilarious "accidents happen" comment, the rest of the class had been drier than his mother's roast chicken, which was so dry it was hard to believe the bird had ever been alive at all.

But finally, the day was over, and he and Mick were headed to the front of the school to meet Kelsey. The front of the school. How awesome was that? No more sneaking out the back to a clubhouse for losers.

Mick trotted up to Devon just inside the main doors of the school. Kids jostled past them, running for buses. For once, Devon didn't find the Friday afternoon buzz in the air annoying. He felt the buzz, too, like little electrical eels skimming over his skin.

He'd noticed that Mick had been acting like he was plugged into a light socket all day. He was jittery and spastic. But Devon understood. He also felt strangely happy about everything. For once, he was enjoying the yellow walls in the school hall (which most of the time reminded him of uncooked egg yolk and made him want to gag). He wasn't minding all the school odors—the chemical smell of the carpet, the dusty smell of chalk, the sweat, the bubble gum, the garlic breath from that day's school lunch. Instead of feeling foreign, it felt familiar.

"Are you ready?" Mick asked, plucking at Devon's sleeve.

Devon grinned. "Ready."

They pushed their way through the double glass doors and both scanned the driveway for a bright red dually truck. Kelsey had been right. They couldn't miss it.

They headed toward it and met up with Kelsey as he trotted over from the gym. "You're here."

Kelsey sounded genuinely pleased. Devon was surprised.

Kelsey raised a hand and waved at a bearded man behind the wheel of the truck. The man waved back, smiling.

Devon wondered what it was like to have an adult male smiling at you. No, seriously, let's tell the truth here. He wondered what it would be like to have an adult male, say, like a *dad,* around . . . period.

The only memory he had of his dad was of an angry man who threw things at his mom. Devon was three when his dad took off. He and his mom had been alone ever since.

Kelsey led Devon and Mick to the pickup. Devon noticed a few kids give Mick and him looks, like they were cavemen who'd escaped the Stone Age. A paper airplane sailed by Devon's head, barely missing his nose; he didn't bother to turn and see where it came from. He kept his gaze on the massive red pickup truck.

"Hey, George," Kelsey said when they reached the truck. He and George did an elaborate finger-flutter into a shoulder bump. "This is Devon"—Kelsey nodded at Devon—"and Mick."

"Nice to meet you, sir." Mick thrust out his hand . . . and dropped the books he'd had tucked under his arm.

Before Devon could reach for them, Kelsey bent down to pick them up.

George, who looked to be a fit sixty-something, shook Mick's hand. "No need for the 'sir.' Call me George." He turned to Devon and offered his hand.

Devon shook it. It was thick and calloused. "Hi, uh, George."

Kelsey stacked Mick's books and handed them back to Mick. Mick shifted them and grinned. "Thanks!"

"Okay," George said. "How about—"

"Hey, Kelsey!" Heather's voice rang out.

Devon whirled to look at her. She was wearing a tight bright red shirt today. He'd spent most of English staring at it, and he was happy to see it again now.

Heather ignored his stare, but Gabriella gave Devon a heavy-lidded look designed to make him feel like a worm. He made an ugly face at her, and she clutched Quincy, who pulled her close and said to George, "Nice rig."

"Thanks!" George grinned and patted the hood of his pickup like it was a dog. "I've got a 6.2 liter V8 under the hood here, 420 horsepower and 460 pounds of torque."

"Whoa," Quincy said. "Sweet." He leaned against the front of the truck like he was posing for an ad. Gabriella giggled and posed next to him.

Devon's jaw clenched.

Quincy and Gabriella were the prettiest people in the school. Gabriella was Hispanic, and she might actually someday get to be the star she told everyone she was going to be. She was that beautiful. Quincy, dark-haired but with lighter skin, had the bad-boy look Devon had once tried to pull off by slicing gashes into his jeans, tearing at his T-shirts, and slouching more. It didn't work for Devon; all he got was a lecture from his mom on taking care of his stuff and standing up straight.

"What are you doing this weekend, Kelsey?" Heather asked.

Kelsey gestured toward Mick and Devon. "We're going to the building supply store to get what we need so we can turn an old workshop into a great hangout spot."

Heather flicked a glance at Devon, then smiled at Kelsey. "That sounds fun. I love DIY."

Kelsey smiled. "That's cool."

Heather laid a hand on Kelsey's arm. "You know, I'm a really good designer. I helped my mom do a surprise man cave for my dad." She turned toward her friends. "Remember building those wall-to-wall bookshelves?"

The three girls laughed, poking one another in delight over some private joke. Devon wanted to throw up. Valerie, a very small girl who wore enough makeup for ten girls, had a nasally voice that turned into a honk when she laughed. And Juliet, tall and slender, had a little-girl giggle that made Devon's teeth hurt.

Quincy pushed off from the truck. "I've got mad hammering skills."

Kelsey looked at Quincy with no expression for a second. Then he smiled and said, "That's great." Devon didn't think Kelsey thought it was great. He seemed annoyed. But why?

Heather took Kelsey's hand. "How about you have a building party this weekend? We can all come and help."

Kelsey opened his mouth, but before he said anything, George grinned and said, "Hey, that sounds great. I can help you set up a barbecue."

Heather gestured at the truck. "Then let's go get some supplies."

Kelsey looked from Heather and her friends to Mick and Devon.

Heather went on. "Quincy's brother was going to take us home, but he had to be someplace. We could go with you to the supply store and then maybe you could run us home?"

"Sure," George said. "Be happy to. But," he looked at the group of them, "you're not all going to fit."

Heather said, "Sure we will. There are only five of us plus you and Kelsey."

"Seven plus me and Kelsey," George said, gesturing at Devon and Mick.

Heather glanced at Devon and Mick. She waved a hand in the air. "Oh, they can ride in the back."

"Nope. Sorry," George said. "That's against the law."

From the moment Heather and her crew had shown up, Devon had felt like he was watching the scene unfold from inside a glass cocoon. He got what everyone was saying, could hear the girls' annoying laughter, but it was all muted. Even though they were standing just a few feet from Devon, they felt very far away, almost like he was watching them on a movie screen. His other senses seemed to have been turned off. He could no longer smell the bus exhaust belching out as the buses accelerated away from the school. He couldn't feel the clothes on his body or the pavement under his feet. Now it felt like fog was rolling into his little cocoon, and it was seeping inside of him, putting his brain in murk that made thinking nearly impossible. Maybe that was why he was surprised when he saw Mick step forward and say to Kelsey, "Um? I thought just me and Devon were going with you today."

Kelsey frowned and looked at everyone. Devon knew the problem. Kelsey was asking himself, "Should I be a jerk and blow off the two losers, or should I ignore the pretty girls?" It wasn't going to be a tough choice. Kelsey was still holding Heather's hand!

George spoke up. "How about this? We'll do two trips.

I'll take some of you kids over there, then I'll come back for the rest. It's only a ten-minute drive. The wait won't be that long."

Kelsey released a pent-up breath. "Thanks, George."

Heather grinned at Kelsey and pulled him toward the pickup's passenger door. "Come on. We can share the front seat. I'm small enough that we can both fit under the seat belt." She giggled.

Kelsey shrugged and let Heather lead him to the front of the pickup. The others piled in the back of the pickup. Quincy pushed Mick back as he squeezed in after the other three girls.

For a second, it looked like George was going to protest the number of kids in the back seat, but then he shrugged and got behind the wheel. All four doors slammed.

George put his window down. "I'll be back for you boys."

As soon as George started his 6.2 liter V8—whatever that meant—engine, Devon's cocoon collapsed. He actually felt his ears pop as the air around him seemed to adjust to real space and time again. His senses went on high alert, too.

The first thing he smelled was the grape soda in Mick's go-cup. Then he got a whiff of gasoline as the big red truck drove away with Devon's short-lived optimism. He knew it was too good to be true.

He felt Mick tug at his shirt.

"Want to sit over there and wait?" Mick pointed at the curb and sucked through his straw. He plunked his padded rump on the curb and piled his backpack and extra books next to him.

A car full of kids blasted past them, and someone let out a shrill whistle. Someone else shouted, "Losers!"

Devon put his back to the driveway. He turned toward the woods and said, "I'm not waiting. I'm going home."

Mick pulled his mouth from his straw. His upper lip was stained purple. "Um? Why?"

Devon glanced down at Mick. He looked pathetic sitting there with his go-cup. Devon wanted to snap at him and walk away, but ten years of friendship and thousands of "in it together" finger links kept his temper somewhat under control. "Seriously? You're asking me why?"

Mick frowned then nodded.

Devon sighed and sat down on the curb next to Mick.

"Do you really think that after the thirty minutes it will take for George to drive them there, come back for us, and then get us there we're going to be welcomed into the group? Don't you think it might be just a little bit, and I'm being very, very sarcastic right now in case you're missing it, *awkward*?"

Mick had to think about that for several seconds. Devon waited.

Finally, Mick sighed. "Yeah, I see what you mean." He sniffed and sucked on his straw. "Why did Kelsey do that? Why didn't he have *them* wait?"

"Again. Seriously? You're asking that? Did you not see him make a move on Heather?"

Mick twisted his lips and looked up out the corner of his eyes as if watching a replay on a tiny screen up and off to the right. He frowned. "I thought *she* made a move on *him*."

"Whatever! He went along when she suggested they share the front seat."

Mick thought that over and nodded. "True."

Devon stood. "So are you coming with me or not?"

Mick sighed. "Yeah, I guess so." He lifted his backpack, and Devon picked up Mick's extra stack of books.

"Does this mean we can't have our clubhouse at Kelsey's house?" Mick asked as they started walking toward the woods.

"Yes, I think that's exactly what this means."

Mick was still feeling a little bummed about what happened with Kelsey when he met Devon for their hike on Saturday morning. He tried not to let things bother him too much. If he did, he'd be miserable all the time. He didn't really want to be miserable.

Mick and Devon lived in a neighborhood that wasn't as nice as Mick wished it was. It wasn't awful; he'd seen much worse. But it wasn't good, either. Left over from when the town was owned by the logging company, the houses in their neighborhood were small, old, and pretty much identical, except for the cars and junk that sat next to them. When Mick and his parents moved into their house, they told Mick it was just temporary—he wouldn't have to share his room with his little sister forever. But he was still sharing his room with his little sister, Debby, something that was bearable only because Debby, who liked to sew, made a curtain to divide their tiny room. That and the fact that they both had earphones and mostly spent their time reading or on their computers kept them from wanting to kill each other.

Sometimes, Mick envied Devon because Devon had his own room, but then he remembered Devon didn't have a dad, not even a lazy dad who never made enough money. At least Mick had a dad, and his dad loved him. That was better than his own room, he guessed.

Mick, his backpack filled with junk food snacks, sodas, water, his little camera, and extra sunscreen, trotted up the cracked and dusty walk to Devon's faded-blue front door. All the houses in the neighborhood had gray siding and blue front doors—some were brighter than others.

Mick was almost afraid to knock on the door. What if Devon wasn't there?

The way Devon had been acting the night before made Mick wonder. Devon was becoming less and less of the friend Mick was used to. It was like something was nibbling on Devon from the inside. It was eating up his smiles and, well, his personality.

Mick blinked when the blue door opened. "Hi, Mrs. Marks," he said to the tall, skinny woman with the short, mussed dark hair. Mrs. Marks wore a pale yellow uniform shirt with dark blue uniform pants. Her brown eyes had circles under them, and her thin lips were pressed together. When she saw Mick, she managed a half smile. "He's almost ready, Mick."

Devon appeared behind his mom. Mick noticed the house smelled like oatmeal and lemons.

"You boys have fun today," Mrs. Marks said.

Devon lifted his backpack and grinned. "We will!"

Mick almost did a double take. Devon sounded downright enthusiastic about their hike. Was the old Devon back?

If so, that would be coolio.

The waterfall was where Mick's dad had promised it would be, and it was as jiggy as he'd promised. The boys found a big flat rock near the base of the falls, just far enough back to be out of spray range but close enough to see the thrashing froth roiling around at the base of the falls. The falls weren't that tall, but they were wide and pretty powerful, probably because it was spring and they were fed by winter snow runoff. Mick loved hearing the water roar as it plunged from the top of the bluff to the stone basin below.

The falls were tucked into a stand of fir trees that enclosed the space around the falls; it felt like the boys were in a lush green cave in a distant land. It was pretty magical, Mick thought. He wouldn't have been surprised if squirrels and chipmunks came dancing out of the woods and broke into song. Of course, he knew that wasn't going to happen, but the falls made it seem possible.

Devon's mood made it seem possible, too. Devon had been pumped up all morning. He had this—what was it? Swag. It was swag. He was acting like he was *all that*. It was looney.

Mick had to admit, though, that he liked this Devon better than the one that had been making him nervous over the last few days. Yes, Devon was still obsessing over that girl, Heather, but at least he was talking and smiling.

Devon stood up and took a picture of the tallest fir tree beyond the falls. "I'm thinking this would make a great location for a scene in one of Heather's movies," Devon said.

"Uh-huh." Mick had no idea what to say when Devon talked about Heather. Pointing out that Heather clearly didn't like Devon didn't seem to do any good. So he was using his mom's "NASAMLN" technique—"nod and smile and make listening noises."

Devon took a couple more pictures, and then he sat down and pulled a package of crackers with peanut butter out of his backpack. He nudged Mick. "I have a surprise for you."

"Did you bring dessert?" Mick had eaten his packaged cupcakes already, and he was still hungry.

Devon laughed. "No. No dessert. Sorry. But I did find us a new clubhouse."

Mick sat up straight. "Really? Where?"

"That's part of the surprise. I did what Kelsey suggested.

I looked for abandoned places near here, and I found one. I'll take you there on Monday after school."

"Why not today?"

Devon grinned in a sly way that made Mick's breath catch for a second.

"It's too far. We have to go east at the railway yard instead of west toward our houses like we usually do."

"Um . . . okay." Why did Mick suddenly feel like Devon was hiding something? He opened his mouth to ask what it was, but then he closed his mouth. Maybe a more subtle approach was needed here. Whatever was going on with Devon, Mick thought it would be smarter to watch and wait instead of meeting it head-on.

Devon finished his crackers, brushed crumbs off his face, and stood. "Come on. I want to scout more locations for Heather."

Mick sighed. "Okay." Stuffing empty junk food wrappers into his backpack, Mick said, "But wouldn't you rather play scavenger hunt?" They'd been playing since they were small, and Mick loved it. One of them would pick an object for them to find, and whoever found the closest thing to it would get a junk food reward from the other. That's how they'd gotten most of the treasures they'd lost when their old clubhouse was torn down. A silver ring became a pop-off tab from a soda can. An airplane became a huge plane-shaped tree branch. A pizza became a big flat rock with pepperoni-shaped speckles on it.

Devon shrugged. "Okay, we can do that, too."

Mick grinned and scrambled to his feet. "Okay. I'll pick the first object. Let's find a fan."

Devon strode ahead. "Sure. Why not?"

It took nearly an hour to retrace their steps from the falls and get back into a familiar part of the woods. It took that long because Mick was running all over looking for something like a fan. When he found a big fern frond, they decided that would do until they located something better. It didn't look like they were going to find something better . . . until a crow pooped on Devon's shoulder.

Mick saw it happen. They were strolling along the fir-needle-padded forest floor, and Devon was juggling three stones as they went. The crow sat on a high branch above their heads. It had cawed when they approached the tree it was in. Mick had looked up at it. As they passed beneath it, the crow flicked its tail feathers and a big white splotch appeared on Devon's shoulder in sync with a squishy, splatting sound.

Mick started to laugh, but then he inhaled sharply as Devon instantly let loose one of the stones he carried, sending it streaking like a missile toward the crow. The stone hit the crow with a stomach-churning *thwack*, and the crow tumbled in what seemed like slow motion to the ground. It landed a few feet in front of them.

While Mick tried to process what had just happened, Devon gestured at the clearly dead bird. "If you want it, a wing would make a better fan," Devon said.

Mick stared at the bird. The forest started to spin around him, and he stumbled back, bracing himself against a tree.

"You okay?" Devon asked.

Mick's mouth was so dry he couldn't speak. Devon started to stroll away, pulling off his shirt as he went.

Mick dug a bottle of water from his backpack and took a big gulp. "Um, I don't need a better fan," Mick said when he found his voice, which didn't sound anything like normal.

Devon shrugged. "Can I have some of your water to clean my shirt?"

Mick handed over his water bottle without speaking. He had no idea what to say. Or maybe he was afraid to say anything at all.

On Monday morning, Kelsey was waiting for Mick and Devon at their lockers. Mick was surprised but pleased. Maybe they'd get to hang out at Kelsey's after all. "Hi, Kelsey," he said.

"Hey, Mick. Hey, Devon."

Mick wasn't sure what to expect from Devon. He knew Devon was mad at Kelsey.

But Devon grinned and smacked Kelsey on the shoulder. Mick noticed Devon had a gauze bandage on his hand, but before he could ask about it, Devon said to Kelsey, "Dude! You have a good weekend?"

Mick felt his eyebrows rising. *Huh?*

Kelsey's brows went up a notch, too. He squinted at Devon for a second. Then he smiled and said, "Look, guys, I'm really sorry about Friday. That was awkward. I wasn't sure what to do. Then when George came back to get you, he said you weren't there. I didn't have your numbers to call you."

"Not a problem," Devon said. "It was awks, and it wasn't your fault."

Awks? Mick had never heard Devon say that before.

Kelsey blew out air. The tentative smile he'd worn since he approached them morphed into a full grin. "I'm so relieved! I thought you guys would be mad at me. You'd have every right to be."

Devon shook his head. "Nah. It's five by five."

Five by five? Mick felt like he was listening to a defective Devon clone.

"Great." Kelsey nodded at several kids who rushed by and waved at him. Then he chuckled and said, "We didn't make much progress on the hangout this weekend. Quincy and Gabriella flaked on me. And . . ." Kelsey looked around. "In all honesty, Heather and her other friends weren't much help." He winked. "But I still don't mind having them around. You know?"

Devon gave Kelsey a close-lipped smile. Then he said, "I know."

Was that a muscle twitch at Devon's jawline?

Before Mick could answer that question in his head, Devon leaned toward Kelsey. "Listen, I've found this place, this abandoned place just like you were talking about. We could actually use that as a hangout instead of your place, or we could just take some of the seriously cool salvage for your hangout. Reclaimed materials make for super-creative spaces."

This is better than a sci-fi movie, Mick thought. *Make for super-creative spaces?* He stifled a laugh.

Kelsey grinned. "Really? You found an abandoned building? That's cool. I never heard back from my buddy. Are you suggesting we do some urban exploring?"

"Exactly," Devon said. "We can meet after school, out back. It's not far. We can walk to it."

"Okay." Kelsey gave Devon a fist bump and broke off to go to his first class.

Devon glanced at Mick. Apparently seeing something in Mick's face, he said, "What?"

Mick shook his head. "Nothing." He still didn't think he should say anything about Devon's strange behavior.

Devon wouldn't have been surprised if Kelsey hadn't shown up after school. He thought Kelsey might suspect something. But nope. Apparently he didn't, because he was already waiting behind the school with Mick when Devon let the thick metal door slam shut behind him. Good. So far so good.

"So where is this place?" Kelsey asked, squinting into the relentlessly bright sun and strolling toward the other boys.

"It's kind of in the woods, about a mile east of the railway yard," Devon said as the boys walked away from the school.

"How come we've never heard about it?" Mick asked. "We've both lived here since we were born," he said to Kelsey.

Devon shrugged. "Don't know."

With Devon in the lead, the boys carefully picked their way through the railway yard, stepping across the rails behind a string of lumbering metal freight cars rolling along the tracks. On the far side of the yard, Devon led them into the woods, and they picked up a winding, uneven trail lined with rotting moss-covered logs and thick clusters of huckleberry bushes and salal shrubs. The air was moist and rich with a loamy smell that made Devon think of rainy days. He liked rainy days for the same reason he liked cloudy days.

Mick and Kelsey chattered as they walked, mostly about TV shows. Mick was going on about a sci-fi show that followed an apocalyptic society in which people were killed for even the smallest mistakes.

"That sounds interesting," Kelsey said. "Kind of up my alley, in an extreme way."

"What do you mean?" Mick asked.

Kelsey shrugged. "Oh, I just mean I like legal shows, courtroom dramas. I'm going to go to law school so I can be a real judge someday."

A real judge? Devon wondered what that meant.

"You don't want to be a builder like your dad?" Devon asked.

"Nope. I like building things, but I'm kind of keen on justice. Dad gets that. He says we all need to do what we're passionate about."

That's true, Devon thought.

About a hundred yards before they reached their destination, the trees thinned, and the sun's rays touched their skin. Devon felt the light and heat hit his face, and for just a second, his feet faltered.

"You okay?" Kelsey asked.

"Yeah. I just tripped."

As fast as it intruded, the sun retreated. Devon turned off the trail and ducked into a denser, darker part of the woods. The other boys followed him.

"Are we there yet?" Kelsey asked . . . then laughed. "My sister always asks that when we're in the car."

"Mine too," Mick said.

Devon ignored them. They were almost there. He led them around a gnarled spruce, and there it was. He stopped and waited for Kelsey and Mick to catch up.

When they did, he heard them suck in their breath in unison.

"Whoa," Kelsey said.

"Creeptastic," Mick said.

Kelsey laughed.

Hunkered in the woods in front of them, a big low-slung building with a shallow roof line and small boarded-up windows clung—barely—to life. Although the building was intact, it sagged and leaned, like it was getting too tired to stay standing. Because a bubble-shaped, filthy but unbroken skylight bulged from the middle of the top of the building, it looked like it wore a bowler hat. It was hard to tell what color the building had been when it was built; now it was mostly green and black, streaked with mold, mildew, and moss. It was also being consumed by wild blackberry bushes. Aggressive, prickly regiments of the vines flanked the building on all sides the boys could see from where they stood. The vines grew low, barely reaching the bottom of the building's few windows, but they were thick, compacted together in a barrier that would demand a blood sacrifice to get past.

"You don't expect us to go through those, do you?" Mick asked Devon.

Devon laughed. "Do I look stupid?" He laughed harder. "Wait. Don't answer."

His laughs were high-pitched, kind of girly. Mick was looking at him strangely.

"Come on," Devon said, leading the boys around the building.

"What was it?" Kelsey asked.

Devon gestured at the wall they were passing. An old, faded sign hung askew from under the weather-worn eaves. The sign was so faded you could only make out an *F*, a *z*, and a *P*. But next to the letters, the image of something round defied the elements.

"Is that a pizza?" Mick asked.

"I think so," Devon said. "I think this was a pizzeria."

"I love pizza," Mick told Kelsey.

Kelsey smiled. "Me too. Hey, Mick, pull out your cell phone and see if you can find anything out about the place. I'd do it, but I forgot my phone at home. I realized it after lunch. I don't think I've ever done that before. I feel naked without it."

Mick laughed and pulled out his phone.

"Don't bother," Devon said. "There's no cell service around this building."

Mick held up his phone and turned in a circle. "Well, that's a little spookeo."

"Come on." Devon motioned for the boys to follow him around the opposite side of the building. When his running shoes started making scraping sounds instead of the dull *thuds* they'd made in the forest, he gestured at the ground. "See? I think this was the parking lot."

"Yeah. Look." Kelsey pointed to the far side of the lot at a sign tacked to a tree trunk. Probably once white, it was now gray, but when Devon squinted, he could see the letter. "Stomers on?"

"Customers only," Kelsey said.

"Should we be here?" Mick asked.

Devon glanced at him. "Why not? Does it look like anyone else cares about this place? Besides, no one ever cared that we hung out in the abandoned gas station."

"He's got a point," Kelsey said.

"Come on over here," Devon said. Although this side of the building looked like it was just as choked by blackberry bushes as the other side, Devon knew better. He stepped over a chunk of broken concrete and bent over. "Do what I do," he said to the others.

Bent almost double, Devon poked his head into what looked like an impassable blackberry bush, but once you got close, it was clear the bush was growing around something. Devon didn't have any idea what the something was, but it had an opening. He dropped to his knees. "You have to crawl," he called back to the other boys.

Mick groaned, but Kelsey shrugged and said, "That's the life of an urban explorer."

Devon grinned. Kelsey was wearing jeans with torn knees. Devon was sure they were the kind you bought already torn, the kind that cost one hundred dollars at least, more than his mom would ever pay for a pair of jeans.

"It will be worth it, I swear. Just go slow," Devon encouraged.

He crawled forward. He knew Mick and Kelsey would follow him. They were too curious not to. After about four feet of tunneling through a narrow opening, he reached the place where he could stand up. So he did, brushing off his legs as he waited for the others.

He looked up and around. He still wasn't sure what this was. It was a rounded enclosure, like some sort of novelty entrance, maybe, to the restaurant. He thought part of the entrance had collapsed, which was what had made for that tunnel-like way in and what had protected this part from the weather and the forest's damp air.

"This is awesome sauce," Mick said, popping up next to Devon. His breath smelled like his favorite grape soda, and his hair smelled like sweat.

Kelsey got to his feet and looked around. Devon noticed one of Kelsey's knees was bleeding.

"What is it?" Mick asked.

"We used to live by the ocean," Kelsey said, "and there was this gift shop that had a shark's head at the entrance. I think this is like that. Not a shark, obviously, but some kind of animal head. See? There are the eyes."

Devon looked up at where Kelsey pointed. He'd missed that when he was here before. To give himself credit, the first time he was here, it was dark. That was Friday evening. He'd wanted to find an abandoned building before Kelsey's "buddy" from his last town could. So he'd headed out after dinner. His mother had fallen asleep on the sofa, as she always did. He'd gone into the woods to explore. He wasn't sure why he went at night. Maybe he'd hoped to get lost. He hadn't really cared. He just wanted to forget what had happened that afternoon.

But instead of being lost, he'd found this place. As he'd explored it, an idea formed. He'd nurtured that idea all day Saturday and through Sunday morning brunch with his mom. When she fell asleep, again, he returned and poked around some more, and his idea grew into a full-fledged plan.

The "eyes" Kelsey pointed out were two round, dirty windows placed where eyes would be if this was, in fact, a head. And the place where the collapsed area lay was where an animal's snout might be.

"I think you're right," Mick said. Mick turned around and gestured at the boarded-up door. He said to Devon, "So now what?"

On the left side of the door, two boards leaned against the wall. Devon reached out and moved the boards, revealing a sidelight window next to the door. The glass in the sidelight was broken out.

"Did you do that?" Mick asked.

"Sure did. Want to take me to jail?"

"Ha-ha." Mick frowned at it. "You expect me to get through there?"

Admittedly, the sidelight was narrow, but Devon had slipped in with no problem, and he figured even Mick could manage it if he sucked in his stomach and they gave him a push. "Yes, I do. That's why I brought this." He pulled from his backpack a roll of duct tape, and while Mick and Kelsey watched, Devon covered the inside of the window frame, which had held the glass, with the thick tape. "This way you won't cut yourself when you squeeze through," he told Mick.

Kelsey stared at Devon for a couple seconds, then said, "Thoughtful."

"Yeah, thanks," Mick said.

That's me, Devon thought, *Mr. Nice Guy.*

When he was done taping, he turned sideways and slid through the opening. Once inside, he called, "Even though that skylight is dirty, it lets in enough light to see, mostly. Mick, why don't you go next? I'll pull if you get stuck, and Kelsey, you push."

"Okay," Mick and Kelsey chorused.

Mick's soft, round shoulder pushed through the opening. He flailed out a hand, and Devon grabbed it and pulled.

"Ow!" Mick protested as he escaped the opening and stumbled to get his balance.

Kelsey slithered through behind Mick. "You okay?"

Mick rubbed his belly. "Yeah."

They all looked around.

"Coolfulness!" Mick said.

They stood in the middle of a huge square room lined with pictures of funky animal characters alternating with crazy and colorful geometric patterns. A domino-like stack of chairs sat against one wall, and another stack of tables lined the other wall. At one end of the room, a stage, its red-velvet and fringed curtains pulled back, presided over the room. And on the stage—

"Creavy!" Mick was rooted to the dirty red linoleum floor, his gaze latched onto the three figures on the stage.

"What is that? A chicken?" Kelsey asked, gawking in the same direction.

"I think so," Devon said.

"Why does it have a cupcake?" Mick asked.

"Maybe it's a baking chicken," Kelsey said and immediately guffawed.

Devon couldn't help himself. He laughed. "Good one."

Mick laughed, too. "Yeah." His stomach growled. "I wish that was a real cupcake."

"Come on." Kelsey walked toward the stage.

Good. He was getting into it. Devon smiled.

He and Mick followed Kelsey to the stage and looked at the figures closely. The figures seemed to be looking back at them, but of course, that wasn't possible.

Devon had to admit he was more comfortable being here today than he had been the day before. Yesterday, he'd been spooked. He only came back today because . . .

"They're animatronic," Kelsey said.

"Yeah," Devon said. "That's what I thought."

"Animatronic? Like robots?" Mick asked.

"Sort of," Kelsey said. "Animatronics can be powered in different ways. Sometimes they use pneumatics or hydraulics, sometimes electricity. Sometimes they're computer-driven."

"How do you know all that?" Devon asked in spite of himself.

"Dad worked on an amusement park resort project once. They had animatronic birds."

"Why a chicken, a rabbit, and a bear?" Mick asked.

"A chicken, a rabbit, and a bear walked into a pizza joint," Kelsey said, and all three boys laughed.

Kelsey was a funny dude, Devon had to admit. Too bad he had to go and . . .

Mick gasped. "Is that a hook?"

To the left of the stage, a cave-like protrusion shrouded in a black heavy curtain announced itself to be Pirate's Cove. Devon hadn't looked behind that curtain. Something about that hook . . .

"Come on," he said. "There's more to see."

Like a short, musicless conga line led by Devon's flashlight, the boys did a tour of the dirty pizza place. When Devon had first explored the pizzeria, he'd felt like he'd dropped into some kind of time warp. Although the interior of the building was damp and there was mildew in places on the ceiling and the walls, it didn't have the trashed look you'd expect in an abandoned building. It seemed like the restaurant had been closed and no one had been inside of it since.

They found the kitchen stripped of its appliances and other equipment, but oddly, it had several jugs of distilled water lined up on the floor by one of the walls. A small office with an old scratched metal desk also had a filing cabinet that was intriguingly locked. If Devon didn't have other plans, he'd want to break it open. Kelsey suggested it, but Devon said they'd get to that later. He led the other boys to a room with banks of control panels and ancient chunky computer screens, and then they visited a couple disgusting bathrooms with broken tile, cracked sinks, and exposed pipes. While they were in the bathroom, Devon was pretty sure he heard something slithering through the walls. He didn't say anything. From the way the other boys' faces paled, he knew they heard it, too. They didn't mention it, either, but they all quickly crowded through the bathroom door and ended up back in the narrow hall.

"The best part is down here," Devon said, motioning the others to follow him.

Devon's heart rate picked up speed. He could almost hear his adrenaline revving at the starting line. He suppressed a smile. Why did he think of that? He wasn't into cars. *6.2 liter V8,* he singsonged in his head.

"Storage?" Mick asked. "This is what you want us to see?"

Devon grinned. "Yeah. Come on."

He pushed the door to the storage room open, shined his flashlight into the room, and stepped back so they could see. It was like looking into some deranged person's closet.

Headless animals hung on long rods that lined two walls of the room. Well, okay, not *actually* headless animals, but headless animal suits. The suits were dingy and dusty. Some were dark with mildew. They all looked stiff and ragged and ratty with fur missing in places. On the opposite wall, three rows of shelves held animal heads—bears and rabbits and birds and dogs. Every head looked a little battered, like it had been used as a bowling ball or something, but the eyes were in place in all of them. They all stared straight ahead like they were lined up for roll call.

"Screepy," Mick said.

Devon looked at Kelsey. Kelsey's eyes were bright. He started poking around in the cabinets that lined the walls on either side of the door. "Look at all this stuff!" he said. He pointed at bins of nails, screws, brackets, wires, and what looked like metal joints. He whirled and grinned at Devon. "You're a genius, Devon. I think I can salvage one of those suits and maybe build our own animatronic character for my hangout."

Devon couldn't help but notice the use of the word "my." Last week, Kelsey had said "our."

A sound similar to rushing water filled his ears. He was pretty sure it was blood racing through his veins in excitement.

"Look over here." He gestured for Kelsey to follow him and went to the back of the room to a small corner closet. His feet made raspy scuffs along the floor that sounded bizarrely menacing.

Devon had found the closet when he was here the first time, partially hidden behind the costumes hung on the inner wall of the room. He'd seen the potential in it, and that had given him his idea. However, it was his second visit that had locked it down, so to speak.

Kelsey glanced at Devon, then grasped the closet's metal handle. Stepping back and to the side, he slowly pulled the door open a few inches. Satisfied nothing was going to jump out at him, he opened the door the rest of the way. Devon's flashlight beam reflected off a pair of big round eyes.

Mick crowded in behind them. "What's that?"

Kelsey reached for the arm of the human-size yellow bear standing in front of them. Devon knew what he'd discover. The arm was heavy.

This wasn't just a furry suit like the ones hanging on the rods. This suit was—

"It's an animatronic suit," Kelsey said. "It has animatronic, um, abilities, I guess, but it can be worn like a costume. I've read about some cutting-edge stuff they're doing with these, where you get in and the suit reads your vital signs and responds to your pulse and temperature and stuff. Some can even respond to specific commands—let the wearer speak in the voice of the character. I'm sure that's not what this is, though. It's too old. I wonder how it works."

He pulled on the arm again. "Let's get it out in the open. I think it will take all three of us."

"Sure," Devon said. "We can do it."

This was going even better than he imagined. He thought he was going to have to talk Kelsey into this, but it looked like he was going to do it all on his own.

It was like it was meant to be.

The three boys grunted with effort, Mick sneezing a few times when dust and tufts of the bear's fur came loose. Working together, they managed to get the bear suit out of the closet and over to the middle of the storage room floor. They lay the bear on its back. Panting to catch their breath, they gazed at the strange character, whose sightless eyes looked straight up at the ceiling in the mottle of Devon's flashlight and the room's dark shadows.

"Let's drag it all out to the main room so we can see it better," Devon suggested.

"Yeah," Kelsey said.

More grunting and sneezing got the yellow bear suit into the main part of the pizzeria. Once they had it in the middle of the floor, Devon knew it was time.

"Mick, why don't you go back and find lids to those bins of screws and stuff. You can stack them up and bring them out. We can take it with us for Kelsey's hangout."

Mick looked over his shoulder at the gloomy hallway. "Take my flashlight," Devon said.

Mick looked back at the bear. Devon could see Mick shudder.

"Okay," he agreed.

As soon as Mick left the room, Devon said to Kelsey, "That bear looks like you."

"Huh?"

"Well, not as cool, but his hair's sort of the same color, and he's smiling like you usually do. If you got this suit working, it could be like the mascot of your hangout."

Kelsey grinned. "That's not bad." He leaned over and took the bear's head in both hands. "Does this come off?" He tugged, and the bear's head released from the suit. He looked into the top of the torso and sniffed. "Doesn't smell too bad, no worse than the rest of the building."

"Nope. I noticed that, too." He nudged Kelsey and grinned. "Try it on."

Kelsey studied the suit's neck opening, then shrugged. "Why not?"

He sat down and started wiggling into the torso. Once in, he said, "This is pretty comfortable." He grinned. "Now the head."

Devon had just clipped on the head when Mick shuffled into the room dragging a stack of plastic bins. "No lids. I'm not sure how we're going to be able to take this stuff out . . ." He stopped and stared at the bear on the floor. He looked around.

"Where's Kelsey?"

"I'm in here," Kelsey called out.

Mick's eyes widened.

"What are—"

Kelsey sat up and said, "I'm not sure how to stand in this thing, but hey, I could waack." He began throwing his arms around in elaborate dance moves.

When he threw both arms straight out to his sides, an ear-stabbing metallic clap resounded off all four walls around them. The clap was followed by a fingernails-on-a-blackboard scraping sound. As abruptly as it started, the scraping sound ended with a loud *SLAP*. This triggered a cascade of snapping sounds, like dozens of steel animal traps springing into place one right after the other.

Kelsey started shrieking with the first snap.

Once, when Devon was little, his mom was driving him to school and she ran over a cat in the street. The cat didn't die immediately. Instead, it made a sound that was like all the sounds of suffering rolled into one—screaming, wailing, howling, and other vocals Devon couldn't even describe. That sonic signature was embedded in Devon's brain. He'd always thought it would be the worst thing he'd ever hear in his life.

He was wrong.

This was the worst.

And the sound wasn't the bad part. It was bad, yes. But the bad part—the really, really bad part—was the way the suit started jerking in a spastic, horrific dance. It looked like the moth-eaten, mildew-blotched gold bear was convulsing.

But it wasn't the bear. Devon knew it wasn't the bear.

It was Kelsey.

What did I do? Devon thought.

"What's wrong with him?" Mick yelled.

Devon jumped. He'd been so mesmerized by Kelsey's suffering that he'd forgotten Mick was there.

Kelsey's shrieks stopped, like someone, or something, had severed his vocal cords. And the suit went still.

That's when Devon noticed it was turning red. Deep, dark, wet red.

"Is that—?" Mick pointed. He dropped to his knees. "That's blood!"

Yeah, that was blood.

Devon sat back on the floor and pulled his feet tight to his body. The blood saturated the bear's matted fur in seconds and began pooling on the floor. Because the linoleum was bloodred, Devon's blood blended with the floor. The only reason Devon could see it was that Kelsey's blood was moving. It had formed an amoeba-like puddle that seemed to be crawling away from the now-saturated bear suit.

Devon stared at the moving blood. It looked like it was a living thing, a thinking red liquid lake stretching out, seeking . . .

Devon scooted even farther away. He groaned and dropped his head into his hands.

This isn't what he meant to do. He'd planned to trap Kelsey in the bear suit and leave him like that for an hour or so to freak him out, as payback for what had happened. If he'd thought for a minute that this is what would . . .

He was angry, yes, jealous. Since Friday afternoon, and maybe even before, he'd hated Kelsey more than he'd ever hated anyone or anything. He'd even hated Kelsey more than he hated his missing dad.

He'd hated Kelsey because Kelsey had everything Devon wanted. Just when it was looking like he had a chance with Heather . . . Okay, maybe he'd been deluding himself about that, but still, he wasn't even given the opportunity to find out. Kelsey swept in and made friends with everyone in, like, two seconds. Devon had been trying for his whole life to make one friend other than

Mick. Kelsey had no right to have everything come so easily to him!

But that didn't mean he deserved this.

"Dev?"

Devon brushed at the tears he didn't realize had formed in his eyes.

"Dev!"

He wiped his face and looked at Mick. Mick was sitting on the floor on the opposite side of the bleeding bear suit. Yeah, sure. Bleeding *bear suit*. Devon was still deluding himself. The bear suit wasn't bleeding. *Kelsey* was.

Devon heard Mick hiccup, and he realized Mick was crying. His dirty face was streaked with tears, giving him a strangely tribal look, like he had vertical stripes of war paint on his cheeks. *Poor kid*, Devon thought. Mick wasn't mature enough to handle something like this.

And Devon was? He barked a laugh.

Mick's gaze, which had been riveted on the bear suit and the flowing blood, whipped to Devon. "Why are you laughing?" His voice was pitched high.

Devon shook his head. "It's . . . never mind. I'm, I think I'm . . . maybe it's shock."

Mick stared at him for a few seconds, then he shifted his attention back to the suit. He flinched. "Look at it. It's still moving. He's still alive. We have to get him out of there."

Devon glanced at the suit. It kind of pulsed, like it was a large bloody heart getting in its last beats.

Mick repeated, "We have to get him out of there."

"We can't," Devon said.

"What do you mean?"

Mick, his mouth hanging open, tears still leaking, his nose running, continued to watch the occasionally trembling suit for . . . how long? Devon wasn't sure.

He didn't feel like he was really there anymore. Obviously, he was. But he wasn't. He was back in his past. He was watching his dad drive away the day he left and never came back. He was watching his tired mother make yet another meal of boxed macaroni and cheese. He was in school watching all the other kids laugh and joke with one another. He was hanging out with Mick in their gas station clubhouse. He was watching Heather, wishing she would notice him. He was relishing the moment when she said his name. He was listening to her talk about justice in social studies class.

He could see her, in her red sweater, and he could hear her tinkling voice: "I think justice is payback."

Payback. That was all he'd intended to do. He'd wanted justice. Payback.

Kelsey had hurt him. He'd made Devon feel like he might be a part of something, and then he'd thrown Devon away. It stung, like being stabbed with a sharp object.

He'd just wanted Kelsey to feel something similar. And maybe he'd wanted Kelsey to end up scarred, like Devon was scarred by every rejection he'd endured.

But he hadn't wanted this. Not this.

"Accidents happen," Heather trilled in his mind.

Devon yelped when Mick shook his shoulder. How did Mick get over here? Devon frowned and shook his cobweb-filled head.

"Why aren't you answering me? I keep asking you what you mean. What do you mean we can't get him out?" Mick was close, too close.

Devon could see snot drying under Mick's nose.

"I mean, we can't because . . ." Devon moaned.

Mick studied him for several seconds, then he slowly scooted away from Devon. "Did you do this on purpose?"

Devon didn't answer him.

"Did you?!"

Devon tried to moisten his mouth enough to swallow.

"Did you *murder him*?" Mick screamed.

"No!" Devon shot up off the floor and started pacing back and forth. Suddenly, tears poured from his eyes, and he couldn't stop them. "No!"

"But what just happened?" Mick hugged his knees and rocked himself.

Devon stared at the bloody suit. He rubbed his face.

"I wanted to get back at him."

"By killing him?!" Mick scrambled to his feet.

"No!"

"Then what?"

"When I was here before, I found the suit, and I tried to put the arm on." His words distorted his sobs, he knew. He could see Mick concentrating, trying to understand him.

"The suit has these locking things inside. Once you snap it in place it's almost impossible to get it off by yourself." Devon tapped the gauze on the back of his hand, where he'd torn off some skin escaping the suit's heavy arm.

"So you *knew* what would happen?"

"No. I mean yes. But no. I mean, I only wanted to scare him! I figured once he was locked in we'd leave him in this place until sundown . . . just to make him sweat a bit! I wanted him to feel something unfair, like what he did to us! Like what I felt when he and his neighbor drove away with . . . I wanted him to be hurt. I didn't want him to actually *get* hurt, though . . . not like that!"

The golden suit shuddered, and Kelsey let out a gurgle.

"He's still alive," Mick whispered. He started toward the suit, but Devon grabbed his arm.

"Don't touch it!"

Mick broke free, stared at Devon for a second, then he ran toward the building entrance. "We have to get help!"

Devon ran after him and grabbed his arm again. "We can't do that!"

"What? Why?"

"We'll go to jail."

"*You'll* go to jail."

"You want me to go to jail?"

"No! Of course not."

"Haven't we always been in it together?"

"Well, yeah."

"We're in *this* together, too." Devon turned and looked at Kelsey and the blood on the floor. The red rivulets weren't spreading as quickly, but they were still moving, crawling like an army of red soldiers across the linoleum.

"We can't possibly get him help fast enough. He's lost too much blood. If we try, we'll only get ourselves in trouble."

Mick stared even harder at Devon. "Are you even sorry this happened?"

"*Of course I am!*" Devon yelled.

Mick held up his hands. "Okay." He took a ragged breath. "Okay."

Devon realized he was shaking. He felt tremors in both of his legs. He had to concentrate to stay standing.

He was a murderer.

A chill skittered along his neck. He wasn't sure whether what he was feeling was because of what he'd done or because he was afraid he was going to get in trouble for what he'd done.

He took a deep breath and squared his shoulders. "Okay. This is what we're going to do."

Mick rubbed his nose and looked up at Devon as if Devon was going to make everything better.

Devon would never be able to make everything better.

"We can't undo what happened," he said.

"*We?*" Mick objected. "You make it sound like I was part of it. I wasn't part of it!"

"Okay. Me. I. *I* can't undo it. So from here, we have a

choice. Either we tell and I go to jail or we don't tell and I don't go to jail. Either way, Kelsey is the same. I wish I hadn't done it. I'm sorry. Very, very sorry. But that doesn't help Kelsey. Me going to jail doesn't help him, either."

"You're saying we should leave him." Mick's voice was hushed.

Devon took a deep breath and let it out. "Yes. That's what I'm saying."

For at least a minute, the boys stood there.

Outside, a crow cawed. Another answered. Inside, the only sounds were those of Devon's and Mick's openmouthed breathing. Both were stuffed up from crying. The uneven and quick huffing sounds they were making were eerie.

But not as eerie as that dry scuttling sound. What was that?

Devon grabbed Mick's arm. "Come on. Where did you leave your backpack?"

Mick pointed. It was against the wall near the entrance, right next to Devon's backpack. Devon made himself turn around and look for his flashlight. It was lying next to the stack of bins Mick had dragged out of the storage room. Making a wide arc well away from the bear suit and the blood, Devon strode across the room and got his flashlight.

"Did you leave anything else?" He tried to ignore the fact that the scuttling sound was coming from the bear suit.

Mick, whose eyes looked glazed, blinked and looked around. "I don't think so."

Devon willed his legs to function right. He still felt like he was shaking all over, and he was still having trouble breathing. But he had to get them out of here. Shoving his flashlight in his backpack, he grabbed Mick by the arm. "Come on."

Devon slipped through the sidelight and yanked Mick through behind him. Mick grunted, but he didn't complain.

Once they'd crawled out into the late afternoon sunshine, though, Mick spoke up. "What about Kelsey's backpack?"

Devon looked back at the building. Should he go get it? And do what with it? No. No one was going to come out here. And if they did and they went in, they'd find Kelsey. Wouldn't they? So what did it matter if his backpack was there, too?

Devon looked at Mick, who was looking around at the woods as if he was trying to figure out what they were. Devon grabbed his arm. "Come on."

Devon was afraid to go to sleep that night. He thought he'd have nightmares.

But he didn't. He was so tired at the end of the day that sleep was like a black void. And the black void was his friend. Not only was it like a blanket of blissful nothingness that wiped out the events of the day, it had a lingering effect the next morning. It acted sort of like one of the sheer curtains his mom had hung in their kitchen. You could still see through it, but it obscured the details.

Tuesday morning, Devon knew what he'd done the day before. He remembered everything, but it was just murky enough to feel unreal, as if he'd watched it on a scary movie instead of living it.

Before he and Mick had split up to head home the previous afternoon, Devon had said to Mick, "In it together."

Mick had repeated the words flatly, like a robot running low on power.

That had worried Devon before he went to bed last night. This morning, he wasn't concerned. Mick would be quiet.

And Mick was, in fact, quiet. Too quiet.

One of the things that Devon had been able to count on for the previous ten years was that his school days would start with Mick chattering. Today, though, Mick wasn't chattering.

The boys were now settling in against the stone wall where they liked to eat lunch outside, and Mick hadn't said more than "Hey, Dev" since Devon had met up with him to walk to school.

Devon was still in a twilight-like state of denial, but the "twilight" was wearing off. When Mrs. Patterson had noted Kelsey's absence from class, the filmy barrier between

Devon and what he'd done tore a little bit. The details were coming back.

Mick opened his lunch sack with none of his usual enthusiasm.

Devon tried to animate his friend. "What did you get today?"

Mick's mom always put in at least one "treat" in Mick's lunch.

"Huh?" Mick sniffed. "Oh. I don't know."

Devon sighed.

Mick set down his sack and leaned toward Devon. He whispered, "I can't stop thinking about him."

"Shh," Devon hissed. "Not here."

Mick's eyes moistened, and his face turned red.

Devon glanced around and then patted Mick's hand. "It's okay. We'll talk about it this afternoon, okay? We'll go to our camp."

He'd hoped the words "our camp" would soothe Mick. Mick liked it when Devon called their makeshift, tarp-covered temporary meeting place "our camp."

Mick wiped his eyes. "Okay." But he said it so quietly Devon could barely hear him.

Settled cross-legged on the cool but dry forest floor, Mick played with a pile of tiny fir cones. Devon watched him, waiting for his friend to speak. He waited for several minutes.

Finally, Mick said, "What if he's still alive?" He

glanced up from his fir cone art, then looked back down. "That's what I can't stop thinking about. What if he's still alive?"

Devon didn't respond. He thought about that, too, but he was sure trying not to.

"I almost puked when they called his name in class," Mick said.

Devon could relate, but he didn't say so. Instead, he said, "I don't think he's still alive."

Mick raised his head and blinked at Devon. "But you're not sure."

Devon shook his head. He could almost hear the ripping sound as the flimsy barrier protecting him from the previous day tore open a little more. He screwed his eyes shut . . . as if that would help.

"No, I'm not sure."

Wednesday. Thursday. Friday.

By Wednesday, panicked fear and mystery rippled through the school like concussive waves radiating outward from a ground zero event. It was all anyone was talking about. Where was Kelsey? The police had been called in.

Mick stayed home from school sick for all three days. When Devon went to see him, Mick swore he wouldn't say anything to anyone. But Mick couldn't keep any food down. His mother thought he had a stomach flu.

Devon handled the whole thing better than Mick. His

years living outside the social groups of the school had given him the ability to keep his face neutral, no matter how he felt on the inside. He was able to go about his business nearly invisibly. He was sure he looked normal . . . even though he was anything but. Every muscle in his body felt rigid. It hurt to move. But he couldn't be still, either. By the end of the week, Devon had nearly chewed his nails off.

On Friday afternoon, Mr. Wright announced to the school that the police concluded Kelsey had run away. Apparently, no one had seen Kelsey leave the school with Devon and Mick, and apparently, Kelsey hadn't told anyone where he was going. Neither one of these things surprised Devon. As far as he knew, only he and Mick left the school the way they did; they were the only ones who ever cut through the railway yard. And of course Kelsey wouldn't tell anyone he was going someplace with Mick and Devon. You only had to be in the school a couple of days to know that it was social suicide to hang out with Mick and Devon. Kelsey was smart enough to have figured that out. Devon was still surprised Kelsey had even apologized to them on Monday. He'd thought it would be much harder than it was to lure Kelsey to . . .

Accidents happen.

Devon visited Mick on Friday afternoon. Mick was eating a bowl of soup when Devon arrived.

"He's keeping his food down," Mick's mom said, giving

Devon a hug in the doorway of Mick's room. "I doubt he's contagious or anything. Go on in."

"Thanks, Mrs. Callahan." Devon smiled at the round, redheaded, freckled woman.

He felt like he had bugs crawling up his arms. It was her hug. He'd felt the same every time his mom had hugged him during the week. He didn't deserve hugs.

"Do you want any soup, dear?" Mrs. Callahan asked. "There's plenty."

Devon shook his head. "Nah. I mean, no thank you."

Mrs. Callahan chucked him under the chin. "You boys are growing up so fast!" She bustled away.

Devon plopped down in the red beanbag chair just inside the door of Mick and Debby's room. "Hey," he said to Mick. He glanced at the bright blue-and-yellow polka-dot divider curtain.

Mick, tucked under a red superhero blanket on his bed, propped up with pillows in matching cases, wiped his mouth. "Hey." He looked like he was going to say something else, but then he went back to eating his soup from a huge orange bowl.

Devon looked around the tiny half room.

Unlike Devon's room, which was pretty bare except for a few nature posters and a couple rock collections, Mick's room was packed full of toys. It didn't look like a fifteen-year-old's room; it looked like a kid's room. Mick's part of the room didn't have much furniture—just a bed, a nightstand, and some shelves with a drop-down desk built in. The shelves held books, but they were also crowded with superhero and sci-fi action figures and stacks of board games.

Devon looked at the curtain again. Mick must have noticed. "Debby's staying over at a friend's house."

Devon nodded.

Mick dropped his spoon. It hit the bowl with a clatter. He wiped his mouth and then said through the napkin he held against his face, "What if he's still alive?"

Devon whipped around to be sure the door was still closed.

"She's in the kitchen," Mick said. "Dad's not home." He shoved his tray away. "I haven't told anyone, and I'm not going to. But I can't stop thinking about him. What if he's alive?"

"It's been six days."

"Yeah, but—"

"He's not alive."

"But he could be."

"How? He can't move. And he doesn't have water."

"How long can people go without water?" Mick asked.

Before Devon could try to answer that question, Mick said, "Wait! There *was* water. In the kitchen."

Devon tensed. Mick was right.

"What if Kelsey managed to get to that?" Mick asked.

"How? That suit was really heavy, and he lost a lot of blood." Understatement of the year.

Mick twisted his mouth and thought about that. "True,

but what if the suit worked with him, like he said some suits like that can. What if it helped him get to the kitchen?"

Devon thought that sounded pretty out there, but what part of what had happened *wasn't* out there?

"If that happened, he could still be alive, and we can't leave him there like that!" Mick leaned forward. "I'll be quiet. I swear. But first, we have to go back and make sure he's, well, you know . . . or not. If he's alive, we have to help him. *We just do.* That's all."

Mick wasn't going to let this go.

"Okay," Devon said. "But *we're* not going. I'll go."

"But—"

"No way is your mom going to let you go into the woods. She thinks you've had the flu. And if you're right, we can't wait any longer. I'll go."

"What if he's alive? How will you get him to a hospital?"

"I'll call someone after I check on him." Remembering the building's cell phone dead zone, he said, "I mean, I'll take bandages and stuff with me so I can . . . what do they call it? Stabilize. So I can stabilize him. What I can do is stay there with him and take care of him until he's better. I can take food and stuff. Then when he's better, I'll leave and go to cell phone range to call for help. That will give me time, too, to convince him not to tell anyone anything."

Mick rubbed his nose and thought this over. Finally, he said, "That's a good idea."

Devon looked at his innocent friend. Mick had no clue.

Devon struggled out of the beanbag chair and went to Mick's bed. He put a hand on Mick's shoulder. "You have to make me a promise."

"What?"

"I don't know how long it's going to take me to get Kelsey out of the suit and help him get well. You have to cover for me."

Mick nodded. "How?"

"I'm going to tell my mom I'm spending a few days here because you need the company since Debby is gone. She'll go for that."

"Okay."

"And if I'm not back by Monday, you have to tell the teachers I'm home sick. Got it?"

"Sure. I can do that."

"And for as long as it takes. Keep telling them I'm sick. Are you sure you can do that?"

Mick nodded.

"No matter what. You can't tell anyone where I am."

"Okay. I'll in-it-together-swear if you want."

Devon shrugged. "Sure." He held out his index finger and listened to Mick's in-it-together-swear that he'd cover Devon's tracks for as long as he needed.

"You're a good friend," Devon said.

Mick grinned.

★ ★ ★

THE NEW KID

When he got home from visiting Mick, Devon told his mom he was going back. "Oh, that's nice of you, kiddo," she said. She looked relieved. Devon figured she was thinking about going to bed early.

Devon went into his sparse room. He looked around. He still wasn't sure what he was going to do when he got back to the pizzeria, but if he was going back, he needed tools.

He sat down on the edge of his twin bed. It sagged under his weight, and he heard one of the box springs groan.

What if he didn't go back at all and just told Mick he'd gone back and found Kelsey dead?

No, he couldn't do it. Even though he'd slept well Monday night, every night since then he'd had nightmares. In every nightmare, Kelsey was a zombie, stalking Devon no matter where he went.

No. He had to go back and be sure.

He picked up his backpack. He pulled his books and phone out of it. He glanced at the phone and sighed. Great. It was dead. *Oh well.* He put it on the charger. He wouldn't be able to use it near the building anyway. He looked around again. His gaze landed on the hammer lying on the floor of his open closet. He'd taken it from his mom's meager supply of tools to fix a shelf a couple weeks before, and he'd never put it away. That would do to open the suit . . . if it came to that.

The sun was starting to sink into the horizon by the time Devon reached the blackberry-choked building. Before he ducked under the collapsed animal-head opening, he got out his flashlight and the hammer.

As he had since he'd entered the forest, he did his best to ignore the rustling, chirring, and crackling he heard in the woods. *Just little forest animals*, he kept telling himself as he nervously ate the chocolate candy bar that would serve as his dinner.

And what would be waiting inside the building?

Taking a deep breath, Devon crawled into the building's outer entrance and then hesitated only a few seconds before slipping in through the sidelight. Once there, though, he froze, shining his flashlight around in jerky spasms.

He half expected Kelsey, in the bloody bear suit, to loom up in front of him and attack. He was poised to escape back through the sidelight.

But nothing came at him. He was alone. Well, alone except for Kelsey's body in the bear suit and the animatronic characters on the stage.

Devon took a tentative step and paused. He listened. The building was totally silent. It felt sinister. Devon had the urge to run even though nothing was moving, nothing was chasing him.

He quelled his fears and moved forward.

Bypassing the blood-soaked bear suit in the middle of the floor, Devon did a tour of the entire building. He went into every room and shined his light in every nook and cranny. He'd watched enough TV to know you "cleared the building" before you let down your guard.

Everything was exactly as they'd left it when they were here on Monday . . . except for the smell. The earthy metallic odor of blood had hit Devon as soon as he'd stepped into the building. Another smell warred with the smell of blood, too. It was sickly sweet, a nauseating smell. Devon was pretty sure it was the smell of decay. But he wasn't sure.

Okay. He'd put it off as long as he could.

With slow, shuffling steps, Devon approached the bear suit. He stopped when he reached the outer edge of the blood pool. It was easy to spot. The blood had blackened as it dried. It was now darker than the floor, and its outlines stood out starkly in the glow of Devon's flashlight.

Gritting his teeth, Devon bent over and touched the edge of the blood. He yanked his hand back. It was still a little sticky.

Okay. That was okay. He was prepared for this. He didn't know how long it took blood to completely dry, but he figured the damp atmosphere of the building would slow down the process.

Devon took off his backpack, and he pulled out the plastic tarp he'd folded and stuffed into it. Instead of bringing the food and bandages he'd promised Mick he'd bring, he'd brought the tarp. He knew Kelsey couldn't be alive, and he didn't want to have to sit in blood to check Kelsey's . . .

Devon made himself stop thinking. He set his backpack against the wall, and he spread the tarp over the blood near the head of the suit.

He had to breathe through his nose because here, the

blood and decay smells were stronger. Kelsey had to be dead.

Devon wouldn't be able to sleep, though, unless he knew for sure.

He trained his light on the bear's head. His muscles stiffened because he expected to see Kelsey's eyes staring back at him through the eyeholes in the bear's head. But . . .

Nothing.

The eyeholes were empty, dark.

Devon leaned closer, aiming the light down into the holes. Why couldn't he see Kelsey's face?

He checked over his shoulder to be sure he was still alone. Had the characters on the stage moved? He sucked in his breath and ran his flashlight's beam over them. He frowned. He couldn't remember how they'd been positioned before. He watched for several more seconds before turning the flashlight back to his task. He put his face closer to the bear's face. He still couldn't see anything.

He'd have to take off the head. That meant touching the bloody fur. Good thing he'd prepared for that, too.

Devon dug into his pants pocket and pulled out a pair of his mother's rubber cleaning gloves. He put them on. Propping the flashlight on the bear's chest to aim it at the neck and hesitating for a second to be sure the chest wasn't moving, Devon felt for the lock mechanism that held the head in place. It took him only seconds to find it. But it wouldn't release. He pushed. He pulled. He pinched. He finally pounded on it with his hammer. But the head wouldn't let go of the torso.

Fine. Devon inserted the claw part of the hammer into the bear's mouth. Using his other hand for leverage, he pried the mouth open.

He sucked in his breath at the ratcheting sound the mouth made when it yawned open. It sounded like teeth gnashing together. Which made no sense. It was opening, not closing.

Letting out his breath, Devon lit up the mouth opening with his flashlight. He tilted his head and looked as far inside the head as he could.

Nothing was inside of it.

Really?

Devon shined the flashlight into the head some more. For sure empty.

Had the bear suit cut off Kelsey's head? *Yeah, and done what with it? Ate it?*

Goose bumps sprang up on Devon's arms because he was reminded of his bounce house story. If a bounce house could eat a toddler, a bear costume could eat a teenager. Right?

"Get a grip," he muttered.

Somewhere in the building, something sputtered faintly. Devon whipped his head around and aimed his flashlight all around the room. It had sounded sort of like a fizzle, like a hoarse exhale. Had it come from behind him?

Or in front of him?

He rotated back quickly so he could inspect the bear suit again. Its bloody fur gleamed in the light, but it wasn't moving.

"Get on with it," Devon commanded himself.

He bent over and directed his light into the bear's mouth again. This time, he concentrated on trying to see down into the torso.

At first he didn't see anything, but then he thought he saw something farther down. Had Kelsey somehow slid down into the suit? Was that his hair that Devon could see? He turned the light this way and that, but he couldn't see any better. He'd have to feel.

Happy for the gloves he wore, Devon squared his shoulders and took a deep breath. Then he slid his arm through the bear's mouth, down inside the bear suit, until all but the uppermost part of his arm was inside. He felt around with his hand, and he still didn't feel anything.

But he heard something. Someone—or something—called his name.

"Devon!"

Devon jerked and started to yank his arm from the suit. But the mouth clamped down on his arm and locked shut with a simultaneous clank and crack. The crack was the bone in Devon's arm.

Devon screamed at the searing pain that shot from his bicep all the way down to the tip of his fingers. Tears sprang into his eyes. He wailed in agony and fear. He also tried to pull his arm out of the bear suit. Bad idea. He howled and held very still. Sweat joined the tears running down his face. Moving his arm was pure torture. It felt like the bear was trying to rip his arm off his body.

Nausea crawled up from his stomach and choked him. He gagged and turned his head to vomit all over his lap. The acidic smell and putrid brown chunky spew made him gag again, and he let loose with another torrent of puke.

Bawling now, Devon yelled for help, even though he knew help wasn't going to come.

"Heeeeeeellllpppp!" The sound he made was even worse than the sound Kelsey had made when the suit had impaled him. It was definitely worse than the dying cat. It was the sound of anguish and despair. It was the sound of hopelessness.

Spittle dripped from his mouth as his cry dissolved into a sob. Ignoring the torment of the lava-hot pain in his right arm, Devon used his left hand to pound ineffectually at the bear's mouth. He kept hitting his arm with the hammer head, and he shrieked every time he did. Still, he kept trying to pound the mouth open.

When he finally lost the strength to hold the hammer and it bounced off the bear's torso and hit the bloody floor with a *thunk*, he started trying to drag the bear suit across the floor. He was out of his head, not thinking logically. He knew he couldn't move the suit.

Collapsing in his own disgusting stink, Devon curled

onto his side, whimpering at every fresh wave of pain that tore through his arm. He tried to ignore the faint sensation of wet warmth trickling down his bicep.

Calm down, he told himself. Mick knew where he was. Mick would come for him.

Devon moaned.

No, he wouldn't. Mick would do what Devon told him to do.

How long did it take to bleed to death? Not long, if he was bleeding a lot, he didn't think. But it didn't feel like he was bleeding much. The trickle of warmth stopped at his elbow joint, and it wasn't moving anymore. No, he wasn't going to bleed to death.

So how long before he died for lack of water? That was what was going to happen. He hadn't brought water because he hadn't planned on helping Kelsey. So now he couldn't help himself.

Inside the suit, he flexed his fingers. He moaned when the movement sent another volley of pain up his arm. Then he froze, sucked in his breath, and clenched his fingers into a fist.

Had he just felt something move inside the suit?

"No, not—" Another slight brush of something moving grazed his knuckles.

"Bugs," Devon whispered. He'd watched enough TV to know about the bugs that liked dead bodies.

It was bugs, right? Not . . . No. It couldn't be . . . Kelsey?

Devon thrashed his entire body, writhing violently in crazed panic. He threw his whole body into it, screaming through the pain the flailing caused in his arm. Vomit sprayed, and the plastic tarp crackled around him. He didn't stop. He fought to free himself with every bit of strength he had.

But it wasn't enough.

In fact, it was making things worse.

After one of his bucking movements, Devon felt his arm loosen for just an instant, but the second it did, it didn't start to come out. It went farther in.

With dread, Devon looked at the suit and realized the mouth had opened farther. The suit was clamped around his shoulder instead of his bicep.

Now he knew. He was going to die here. He couldn't get his arm free, and he couldn't move the suit. And Mick was going to be sure no one came for him. Mick had disagreed with Devon plenty of times over the years, but he never went against Devon. Not one single time.

Devon thought about the movie he saw where the man sawed his arm off to free himself when he got his arm caught under a boulder. He gagged and retched. Not a good thought. And not helpful, either. Even if he had a knife or a saw, he didn't think he could do that.

Devon wiggled in one more attempt to free himself. The mouth opened even more, and Devon got a sudden glimpse inside the suit.

He gasped, and for a moment, shock blocked his pain.

Down low, past his arm, Devon could see a body, a dead body, just like he thought he'd find when he came back here to check. But it wasn't *exactly* like he thought he'd find. The body he thought he'd find didn't have blond hair. This one had curly black hair.

The body in the suit wasn't Kelsey.

Devon only had a second to try to make sense of this before his shoulder was sucked into the suit. Devon screamed, but no one heard him.

On Monday morning, Mick was disappointed when Devon didn't meet Mick to walk to school. Mick hoped he'd find Devon waiting for him at the lockers, waiting to tell him Kelsey was going to be okay, or even waiting to tell him Kelsey was dead. That wasn't as good, but it would be better than the way they'd left things last week. Not knowing whether Kelsey was dead was like being eaten alive, like getting digested by that creepstyle bounce house in the story Devon read in English class a couple weeks ago.

Was that just a couple weeks ago?

Speaking of English class, Mick was supposed to read a poem out loud today. Remembering that made his stomach churn. It twisted up his insides so much he didn't worry too much about Devon not being in school. Devon had told him it might take a while to get Kelsey well enough to move him. Something about that seemed . . .

Someone bumped into Mick, and he dropped his backpack. He bent over, picked it up, and went to class.

In English class, Mick was reading his poem over and over while Mrs. Patterson did roll call. He was so into it he jumped when Mrs. Patterson called out, "Mick!"

"Here!"

"Yes, I know you're here. I asked you if you know where our budding horror writer is."

"Huh?"

"Devon. Where's Devon?"

"Oh, sorry. He's home sick."

"Okay."

Mick smiled. He'd done his part.

In it together, for as long as it takes.

Kelsey leaned against a column in the rotunda of his new school. He watched the other kids, and he smiled or nodded at everyone who passed him, saying, "Hey" when someone said hello.

His gaze kept returning to a couple of boys who lingered outside the front doors of the school. One of the boys wore all black; the other wore ragged jeans and a faded T-shirt. Other kids coming into the school ignored the boys or gave them scathing looks. Both boys occasionally snickered at the passing kids.

Kelsey pushed off from the column and strolled toward the boys as they finally sauntered into the school. He stopped in front of them and said, "Hey, I'm Kelsey, I'm new here."

Both boys eyed him, brows raised.

He gave them each a big friendly grin. "So," Kelsey said, "any cool places to hang out around here?"

ABOUT THE AUTHORS

Scott Cawthon is the author of the bestselling video game series *Five Nights at Freddy's*, and while he is a game designer by trade, he is first and foremost a storyteller at heart. He is a graduate of the Art Institute of Houston and lives in Texas with his wife and four sons.

Elley Cooper writes fiction for young adults and adults. She has always loved horror and is grateful to Scott Cawthon for letting her spend time in his dark and twisted universe. Elley lives in Tennessee with her family and many spoiled pets and can often be found writing books with Kevin Anderson & Associates.

Andrea Rains Waggener is an author, novelist, ghost-writer, essayist, short story writer, screenwriter, copywriter, editor, poet, and a proud member of Kevin Anderson & Associates' team of writers. In a past she prefers not to remember much, she was a claims adjuster, JCPenney's catalog order-taker (before computers!), appellate court clerk, legal writing instructor, and lawyer. Writing in genres that vary from her chick-lit novel, *Alternate Beauty*, to her dog how-to book, *Dog Parenting*, to her self-help book, *Healthy, Wealthy, and Wise*, to ghostwritten memoirs to ghostwritten YA, horror, mystery, and mainstream fiction projects, Andrea still manages to find time to watch the rain and obsess over her dog and her knitting, art, and music projects. She lives with her husband and said dog on the Washington Coast, and if she isn't at home creating something, she can be found walking on the beach.

L arson sat at the elegant oak rolltop desk that dominated one end of his otherwise anything-but-elegant living room. If he sat at the desk, the top of which held an antique green banker's lamp and above which hung a print of an eagle flying over a meadow, his back was to the rest of the room. From here, he could pretend the other part of his living room didn't exist. Everything else in the room—the stained card table, two folding chairs, a ratty easy chair, and a blue vinyl beanbag chair—only made the place seem more empty and sad.

Taking a sip from the glass he held balanced against his chest, he looked at the framed picture of Ryan that the banker's lamp illuminated. Ryan had been six when the picture was taken. He'd just lost his front two baby teeth. The resulting gap gave his freckled, blue-eyed face an impish look Larson loved. People said Ryan was the spitting image of his dad. Larson guessed he saw it. For sure he and his son shared dirty blond hair, freckles, blue eyes, and a wide mouth. Ryan had gotten his mom's nose, which was good for Ryan. But sometimes, all Larson saw when he looked at his son were the differences between them. To Larson, his own face looked hard and closed, while Ryan's was still eager and open.

How long would it stay that way?

A few days before, Larson had gotten a glimpse of what Ryan would look like when the possibilities of childhood collapsed into the obligations of adulthood. Larson had promised, swearing on a stack of comic books no less, that he'd take Ryan to see a movie premiere. Work had gotten in the way, and Larson had canceled. Ryan hadn't taken it well.

"You don't do anything you say you'll do!" Ryan had screamed. His face was red and contorted with crushing disappointment.

"I'm sorry, Ryan."

Ryan had sniffled. "Teacher says dads are like superheroes. But you're not. Superheroes don't break promises."

Larson's phone rang, and he snatched it up. Anything that could save him from the memory of his many regrets would be welcome.

"The Stitch Wraith was spotted again," Chief Monahan rasped. "I want you to get over there."

"Where?"

"The old fire site . . . you remember that bizarre fire?"

"Sure." Larson set down his drink, glad he'd only had a

couple sips. "I'll be there in ten." He stood. "Wait. Isn't that the second time it's been spotted there?"

Don pulled open the heavy metal door of the old ex-factory, and he and Frank headed to the food truck parked in the middle of what used to be one of the defunct factory's assembly rooms. The truck, no longer mobile, was permanently placed in the room, and it was surrounded by wood picnic tables. It was a weird setup, but then, Dr. Phineas Taggart, the man who owned it all, was weird, too.

Don spotted Phineas sitting on one of the picnic table benches, and he nudged Frank. They watched Phineas carefully pull the tail of his pristine white lab coat out from under him and smooth it, then just as carefully spread a white linen napkin on the rough table in front of him. He flicked a speck of dirt from the napkin's corner, then opened his sandwich wrapper in the precise center of the napkin.

"Thank you," Phineas said to the sandwich. "Cells, please process this food with love."

"Still talking to your food, Phineas?" Don called. He rolled his eyes and winked at Frank.

Frank just shook his head.

They watched Phineas close his eyes. It looked like he was praying, but he'd once told them he was creating a "mental shield out of light" when he did that. Whatever that meant.

"Hello, Don," Phineas said. "As I have previously

explained, I am not talking to my food per se. I am talking to cells, both the cells in the food and those of my body."

"Right, right." Don nudged Frank again. "Can you say one sandwich short of a picnic?" he muttered to Frank.

Frank, who had the same darkly tanned face and forearms and broad thick shoulders that Don had, set his hard hat on the picnic table next to the one Phineas sat at, and he stepped over to the food truck to order his food.

"How's that 'shield' coming?" Don asked, dumping his hard hat next to Frank's. Phineas watched Ruben scribble down Frank's order, then he looked at Don.

"I am developing a modicum of expertise with shield creation," Phineas said.

Frank returned from ordering and plopped on the picnic table's bench. Dust billowed up from his thighs when he sat. Don noticed Phineas's nose twitch. He probably wasn't thrilled with how sweaty he and Frank smelled. Phineas was a little prissy.

"You gotta hear this, Frank," Don said. He nodded at Phineas. "Tell him."

Phineas looked at his sandwich, but then he straightened his narrow red tie and adjusted the stiff collar of his gray dress shirt. He cleared his throat. "The creation of a personal field has its origin in the work of a psychologist who did a series of experiments on the effect of being stared at."

"Why would anyone study that?" Frank asked.

Don, who stood at Ruben's counter ordering his food, said, "I hate being stared at. Makes my skin crawl." He loved winding Phineas up and listening to him spout off about all the weird stuff he was into.

"Precisely," Phineas said. "That's why this psychologist was studying the phenomenon. Why does it bother us when people stare at us? To measure the test results, the psychologist used EDA—electrodermal activity—readings. The readings show responses of the sympathetic nervous system."

"That makes perfect sense," Don lied. He winked at Frank, who grinned.

Phineas was oblivious to their amusement. He continued his informational download. "The results of his experiments were that those being stared at showed significantly higher electrodermal activity when they were being stared at than would have been expected by chance."

Frank shrugged. "So what?" He rolled his eyes at Don, who chuckled.

"So," Phineas went on, "this man did other experiments as well. He wanted to know if it was possible for people to influence others with negative intentions. If it was, could one protect oneself from these negative intentions?

"He conducted more experiments, in which one group of subjects was given no instructions and another group was instructed to visualize a protective shield or barrier that would protect against interference of another person's mind. The experimenters then attempted to raise all of the subjects' EDA levels by staring at them and willing the levels to rise. The result was that the group that had shielded themselves showed far fewer physical effects than the other unshielded subjects."

"So will your shield stop speeding bullets?" Don laughed as he took his grilled ham and cheese from Ruben.

Phineas smiled. "Speeding bullets aren't nearly as dangerous as human emotion." He picked up his sandwich and took a bite.

Frank snorted. With his mouth full, he said, "That's just stupid. My neighbor's anger can't leave me gut-shot, but the old lady's shotgun can."

"You're looking only at the short-term timeline," Phineas said. "You see the result of the shotgun's energy, so it seems greater to you. Human emotion is slower to impact, more insidious. It emanates from us or is excreted from us, if you will, like sweat or tears, and it wafts outward like a noxious cloud, soaking into the surroundings. For some time, I have been studying the effect of these emotions. I am getting close to a breakthrough."

Phineas left his ersatz friends by the food truck and returned to the main part of the ex-factory—his private area. He wished the food truck was his private area, too, but alas, Ruben wouldn't agree to that.

When Phineas used to work at Evergreen Laboratories, Ruben's food truck used to be parked outside the ugly concrete building that housed the labs. When Phineas retired, he asked Ruben to set up shop in Phineas's factory-converted-to-laboratory because he loved Ruben's food. Ruben agreed, only if he could remain open to the public in general. Hence the presence of men like Don and Frank. Phineas knew that they, and others, thought he was nutty, but he still occasionally enjoyed their company.

Phineas brushed his teeth after lunch and made sure he still looked spiffy. Being retired was no excuse to get sloppy. So Phineas still dressed as he had for work, and he still kept his graying hair trimmed short and his round homely face clean shaven. When he was growing up, his mother told him, "Being ugly is no excuse to be a slob." She also frequently asked him, "What do you need looks for when you have such a brain?"

Phineas agreed with his mom, which was why his life's work—not the pointless pharmaceutical work he did at his job, but his true calling—was the study of the paranormal, the study of energy and its effects on all matter, animate and supposedly inanimate.

Satisfied that he was presentable, Phineas left the bathroom and walked down the narrow hall to his Protected Room. Punching in his security code and deactivating the pneumatic seal that guarded his treasures from errant energies such as those of mold spores and the like, Phineas entered the all-white room of shelving and glass cabinets. Indulging himself, as he did daily, he strolled up and down the rows looking at his accumulated bounty.

Phineas knew that to the untrained eye, the items in this

room would look like either rubbish or the collection of a horror movie aficionado. It all depended on perspective. Only Phineas knew that every item in this room was said to be "haunted."

"Haunted" was not a term he himself used. Usually used as a word to refer to something embodied by a ghost, the word could also mean part of what Phineas knew to be true of all things. "Haunted" could mean showing signs of torment or some kind of mental anguish. And this was the more important definition of the word. These items on Phineas's shelves weren't possessed by ghosts; the ones that were truly haunted were energized by agony.

The rack, the head crusher, the wheel, the Judas cradle—these torture devices were some of the purest examples Phineas had collected, but he also had everything from the Madonna's image on toast to nonmechanical dolls that opened their eyes by themselves to a rocking chair that rocked on its own. He'd acquired all of these special objects from online auctions. He loved each and every one of them.

But he couldn't linger here all day. He had work to do.

Exiting the Protected Room, Phineas returned to his small office, where a laptop computer sat in the middle of a simple oak desk. There, he began to type up his latest findings.

"As I expected," he typed, "extreme human emotion appears to impact its surroundings far more powerfully the more negative it is. Agony, I'm convinced, radiates farther from people than any other emotion. Love has its influence, but the experiments being done with water crystals have been misinterpreted. Just because love forms beautiful ice crystals doesn't mean it's the most powerful emotion. Yesterday, I mimicked the ice crystal methodology, and by allowing all the hurt and anger I usually keep well in check to burst forth, I watched water manifest a hideous crystal in a matter of seconds."

Phineas stood and crossed to the grow light over his collection of exotic flowers. He ran his fingertips over the lobster-claw-shaped yellow and orange Heliconia, the satisfyingly symmetrical lavender Lotus flower, the red clusters of flowering ginger, and the brighter red perfumed passionflowers that reminded him of blood-soaked starfish.

Other researchers had their water. Phineas had his flowers. He believed flowers, not water, were nature's purest vessels for emotion. He was drawn particularly to the passionflower because the passionflower was known to hold a vibration so pure and innocent that its energy could repattern consciousness. Phineas leaned over and inhaled the flower's pungently sweet scent. This flower, he'd learned from an expert in flower-energy essences, was known to repair the ego. It could literally mend the superego and facilitate enlightenment. He believed that he was approaching the day when he was so attuned to the flow of his own energy that he could get in resonance with this extraordinary blossom.

But not now. Phineas checked his watch. It was time.

★ ★ ★

Every week, Phineas received a new shipment of emotionally charged items. This week, he had some very special objects coming.

Hurrying down the hall to the loading dock at the back of his old brick factory, Phineas practically skipped over the stone floor. He couldn't wait to see his new purchases.

"Yo, Phin," a burly bald man called when Phineas stepped onto the concrete platform.

"Hello, Flynn." Phineas bounced on the balls of his feet and rubbed his hands together. He leaned forward to peer into Flynn's truck. "What have you?"

Flynn leaned over and picked up a box. He grinned. "You're putting me on. You know what you've ordered. Today's the special day, right?"

Phineas laughed.

Flynn leaned back and widened his warm brown eyes. "Whoa, doc. That's some mad scientist evil laugh you got there."

"Do you like it? I've been practicing."

"Nailed it." Flynn, his pink head glistening in the sun and his back muscles rippling under his black T-shirt, began unloading boxes onto the dock.

Phineas didn't bother explaining to Flynn that Phineas didn't even have a natural laugh. One of the reasons he was so fascinated by the bandwidth of human emotion was because he could never seem to access the whole range of emotions himself. He didn't have a natural laugh because he'd never felt real joy.

What he felt now, though, had to be close. Flynn unloaded the fourth box from Phineas's shipment, checked his manifest, and said, "That's it, doc. Let me just get the handcart, and I'll take this stuff back to your lab."

"Thank you, Flynn." Phineas was careful not to add a "hurry up," even though he wanted to. Flynn wasn't dawdling. Phineas was just impatient.

Flynn tossed the handcart onto the dock, then jumped up and stacked the boxes. The tower was over his head, but he said, "Got it" and went off down the hall, holding the top two boxes on the cart with his left hand as he pushed the cart with his right. Phineas scurried after him.

It only took a few seconds to reach the main lab, which was the vaulted core of the factory, what had once been the factory floor. Previously full of automated assembly equipment, this space was now home to Phineas's various methods of measuring energy. Like Braud, he had his EDA. He also had his EEG, his REG, his MRI, and his X-ray machines. He'd used all of them at one time or another in experiments designed to measure the emotional energy left behind in objects that had been near the site of a tragedy.

"Right here, Flynn." Phineas pointed at two large bare tables, and Flynn shifted the stack of boxes to the floor between them.

He gave Phineas a salute. "Have a good one."

"I will."

Before Flynn had taken a step, Phineas was tearing into

the first box. Peering into it, he saw a stack of party plates. "Wonderful," he said.

He opened the second box, which was flat and oblong. When the box was open, Phineas found himself staring at his own reflection. This was the decorative wall mirror that had watched a man murder his entire family. *Oh, what agony might this contain?* Phineas ran his hands over the shiny surface.

Then he took a deep breath and opened the large square box. As he suspected, this box contained yet another box—an empty jack-in-the-box box. Wonderful. This was going to have a lot of juicy agony in it.

And last but not least . . . yes, there it was! Lying in a puffery of Styrofoam peanuts, a man-size endoskeleton lay, just waiting to be activated and given a purpose.

Phineas lifted the endoskeleton from the box, and he frowned when it hung limply in his arms. He hadn't expected it to be this broken. Well, no matter. At the moment, it looked like nothing—just a ruptured metal network made to stand in for human bones. But it wouldn't be nothing for much longer.

"Don't worry," Phineas said. "I'll provide."

Phineas got right to work. Hooking together the lines and electrodes of his various energy-measuring devices, he set up what he thought of as an energy cascade. The machine would pour energy already captured from previous items into the first new item—in this case the plates—and then usher that energy through all the additional new items until they culminated in the endoskeleton.

Phineas stepped back to watch the process. Not that there was anything to see. Unfortunately, the transfer of emotional energy occurred at a frequency the human eye couldn't discern. If Phineas turned out all the lights and used a blue light, he could detect just a bit of the energy flow. He'd discovered, however, that blue light tended to distort the field. He couldn't risk turning it on now.

Instead, heeding his growling stomach, Phineas decided to return to the food truck for an early dinner.

"How is your daughter doing?" Phineas asked Ruben while Ruben fried the portobello mushroom for Phineas's veggie burger.

Ruben shrugged, his black ponytail swaying. "Still painfully shy."

"I could give you a remedy for that, a flower essence called Mimulus."

Ruben leaned on the counter and cocked his head with a smirk. "What's a *flower essence*?" He made it clear he was poking fun at the idea.

Phineas disregarded Ruben's tone. "In the early part of the last century, a homeopath discovered that diluted energies of various plants and flowers had an impact on emotion and the physical body. A flower essence called Mimulus transforms fear into strength."

"So a flower would make her less shy." Ruben shook his head and looked up at the ceiling in what even Phineas could tell was a "Now I've heard everything" expression.

Phineas ignored the dismissal. "Not exactly. The *energy* of a flower would make her more confident. Only a molecule or two of any given flower is suspended in a solution of water and alcohol for each flower remedy."

"Oh crap." Ruben realized he'd burned the mushroom. "Sorry." He started over. "So, is that what you're working on? Flower . . . energies?"

"Not quite." Phineas straightened and clasped his hands. "You see, I'm convinced that agony has a greater energetic radius and power than any other emotion. I have done numerous experiments to measure, capture, contain, and study the leftover emotion embedded into objects that were near a tragedy. My work is focused on my hypothesis that you can take a saturation of agony, add any kind of intelligence—even an artificial one—and they will combine together to transmute the energy of emotion into the energy of physical action. This, I believe, is what explains what people call 'haunted' objects."

Ruben laughed, shook his head, and managed to properly cook Phineas's portobello. "No disrespect, doc, but I'm glad I don't believe in magic. Your flower essences sound like hocus-pocus. But the rest of that stuff you just said; that's even worse—it's bad mojo."

"Maybe," Phineas admitted. "But maybe it's the key to understanding the energy of all things."

By the time Phineas returned to his lab, the endoskeleton lit up like a Christmas tree when Phineas tested its energy levels. It was ready. Now he just needed to give it a bit more presence so it could properly express the agony it had soaked in from the other items.

Phineas hurried to his Protected Room. He knew exactly what he needed, so it only took a few minutes to place the items in separate boxes and return to the lab. There, he put the boxes on the table next to the bare endoskeleton.

Running his hands over the metal skeleton, he reveled in the electric energy dancing at his fingertips.

"First, a head," he whispered.

Reaching into the first box he'd set on the table, Phineas pulled out a three-foot-tall white doll covered in drawings done in colored markers. The doll was truly an abomination of decorative overkill. It had rainbow fingertips, green knees, brown smudges on its body and legs, and various bibs and bobs glued to it, one of which appeared to be a smiley face eraser. Uninterested in the doll's body, Phineas grabbed the doll's flat black-marker-drawn face and pulled it from the doll's neck. He then affixed the head to the top of the endoskeleton.

"That's better," he said. "Gives you some personality."

He reached into the second box. "And now for some heart."

The item in the second box was an animatronic dog that clearly no longer functioned. Phineas set his shoulders and prepared himself to touch it. The dog was an ugly dog, as ugly as Phineas himself, what with its matted grayish-brown fur, triangle-shaped head, and wide mouth full of sharp teeth. But it wasn't just ugly. It was *wrong* somehow. Of all the items in Phineas's collection, he found this dog to be the most menacing. He sensed the dog had been responsible for some powerful agony. He'd never been entirely comfortable having it around. But now he was going to take it apart, so it wouldn't be a threat.

Using sharp shears, Phineas tore into the dog's fur. Then he used pliers to pull out wires and circuitry. In minutes, he'd revealed the dog's battery pack, located in the dog's chest where its heart would have been had it been a living dog. Lifting the large plastic-encased unit trailing a tangle of entwined wires, Phineas studied the endoskeleton. Where to install it? Phineas dismissed plug-ins in the endoskeleton's head and neck and instead found a suitable port in the endoskeleton's chest.

He grinned when he looked at it. "Ha. There. Now my Tin Man has a heart." He chuckled.

The moment the endoskeleton got its heart, it became more than an endoskeleton. It became an animatronic being of great energy. And it moved.

Phineas laughed, genuinely laughed, in pure glee.

The being of great energy reacted to Phineas's laugh by turning to look at Phineas with its black marker eyes. Phineas kept laughing, and the being reached out to touch its creator.

Phineas held his breath as the metal fingers met his skin. Then, in one crowded instant, three things happened:

Phineas saw the being's battery pack pulse bright red. He suddenly sensed danger and attempted to throw up a mental shield. He began to convulse, grabbing his head to attempt to contain the excruciating pain that annihilated his consciousness.

Although Phineas owned the building where Ruben ran his business, Ruben thought of the cavernous room that held his truck and the picnic tables that surrounded it as his own space. The rest of the building was Phineas's space, and Ruben had never gone into Phineas's space. It wasn't that it was off-limits. It simply seemed impolite to wander into Phineas's domain.

This afternoon, though, Ruben thought he had to venture into the heart of the old brick building. He was worried about Phineas.

In the two years since he and Phineas had reached their agreement, Phineas had never missed a meal at Ruben's truck. Today, he'd been absent for both breakfast and lunch. Something was wrong.

So Ruben went where he'd never gone before, and in minutes, he'd discovered why Phineas had missed his meals.

Phineas was dead.

He was not only dead, he was withered into near mummification, his mouth gaping open, his eyes gone.

When Ruben found Phineas, he immediately staggered back to his truck. He called the police, who came, investigated, and announced that they suspected some kind of electrical discharge killed Phineas.

Ruben wasn't so sure. He spent the rest of the day trying not to see Phineas's body in his mind's eye. He didn't want to see that or the weird lab with its wilting exotic flowers. He especially didn't want to see the black tear streaks that had stained the dead scientist's face.

In the middle of the stack of Phineas's belongings on Flynn's truck, the energetic being lay under a large heavy tarp that smelled like turpentine. Its metal extremities vibrating with the rumble of the truck engine, the being sat up. Turning, it surveyed its surroundings until its gaze landed on a pile of clothing.

The being grabbed a cloak from the pile and slipped it on.

A DEADLY SECRET IS LURKING AT THE HEART OF FREDDY FAZBEAR'S PIZZA...

Unravel the twisted mysteries behind the bestselling horror video games and the *New York Times* bestselling series.